SOLDIER OF FORTUNE

FORTUNE CHRONICLES 1

KATHLEEN MCCLURE

PUBLISHED BY OUTRAGEOUS FICTION

First edition edited by Claudette Cruz
Second edition edited by Lori Diederich
Cover by Youness Elh

ISBN:
978-1-947842-33-5 (eBook)
978-1-947842-34-2 (Paperback)

More Outrageous Fiction

THE FORTUNE CHRONICLES

Soldier of Fortune

Fortune's Fallen

Outrageous Fortune

Change of Fortune

Fortune's Fool

THE ZODIAC FILES

The Gemini Hustle

The Libra Gambit

Thank you for choosing *Soldier of Fortune*.

If you enjoy the journey, please consider leaving an honest review. For individual creators like me, your feedback is the best way to help other fans of quirky science fantasy discover our worlds.

And for more outrageous fiction, including new stories, exclusive content, and reader community, scan the QR code below to follow our Outrageous Crew on Ream. It's free, easy, and the best way to delve into our fantastical worlds!

Happy reading,

Kathleen

https://reamstories.com/outrageouscrew

About the Fortune Chronicles

The Fortune Chronicles are a series of standalone adventures featuring a colorful cast of characters who wander through each other's narratives from time to time.

We hope you enjoy your visit to the distant future and the planet Fortune, where tech is low, tensions high, and heroes unlikely.

For Sam.
Here's looking at you, Kid.

All warfare is based on deception.

— SUN TZU

CHAPTER I

Morton Barrens
Maximum Security Penitentiary
United Colonies of Fortune
February 9, 1449 After Landing

GIDEON QUINN CONSIDERED THE CARDS IN HIS RIGHT hand. Given said cards were so faded he could barely see the original suits, and since what *was* visible tended to waver in the glare of the setting suns, they required some serious considering.

While he considered, his opponent—a Nikean the outside world had known as Dr. Ephraim Rudd, but in Morton answered to "Doc," "Prisoner 64326," or, "Hey, you!"—shot one finger out to catch the drop of perspiration sliding from his nose, and brought it to his tongue.

Gideon, long since sweated dry by the day's labor, tried not to envy Doc the pittance of moisture.

The two men were perched on opposite sides of the sandstone slab which served as their table. Both were near in height, though Gideon topped Doc's lanky frame by an extra few centimeters. Both were also tanned by the unrelenting suns of the Barrens, and both bore touches of silver in their hair, despite the fact that Gideon was at least a decade younger than Doc.

Though they shared the genetic trait of blue eyes, Doc's were of a soft, lake-like hue, while Gideon viewed the world through eyes as sharp and dangerous as live crystal.

They both also had the look of men who lived on the prison's notorious rations, but where the doctor merely looked underfed, Gideon's spareness was of a harder, more feral nature, as if all excess had been burned away by the same suns that left him covetous of another man's sweat.

"Anytime, now," Doc prompted as, a dozen meters away, a slap of wood against pineapple leather was followed by the cheers of a team who'd scored a goal in an evening game of net the queen. A short cackle drifted from a pair of inmates walking the circumference, and on the far side of the yard, nearest the cell blocks, a wail of sorrow rose from where Lonnie's theatrical troupe was rehearsing a production of *Dream of the Red Chamber*.

At least it wasn't *Romeo and Juliet*, Gideon thought. "I'll see your bet, and raise," he said to Doc as the cheers of the queen players receded.

"Raise with what?" Doc gestured to the pot, in which Gideon's three ration bars and an old newspaper shared the space with six of Doc's tea packets and a tin of mint pastilles. "Since I'm fairly sure I see all your worldly goods before me. Unless you're willing to put Elvis in the pot?"

Hearing his name, the draco currently stretched on the hot sandstone next to Gideon's thigh raised one of his lids.

"Elvis is off the table." Gideon gave his reptilian companion a gentle scritch between the folded wings until the half-open eye closed again. "Okay, technically he's on the table, but you know what I mean."

"I think I can grasp the metaphor," Doc replied with a smile before continuing. "But that still leaves the question of what you have to bet?"

In response, Gideon produced a thin sheaf of grubby pages from his back pocket. "Got chapters six through nine of *Curse of the Amazons*," he said, laying the wrinkled pages on the table. "Good enough?"

"Honey from the keepers," Doc judged, eyeing the well-worn pages of the melodrama with anticipation. "Call."

"Quinn!"

Gideon's eyes darted up to spy two corrections officers approaching. Dust puffed like red smoke as they crossed the yard, giving the illusion of walking through fire.

"Warden wants you upstairs," CO Milton, who was new to the Barrens, barked, startling Elvis.

"Can't it wait?" Gideon soothed the hissing draco with one hand and waved his cards with the other. "I'm sitting on an apiary, here."

"You're sitting on a full hive, at best," Doc reproved mildly.

"Only one way to find out." Gideon grinned at the other man.

"Cut the crap, Quinn." CO Finch spoke with the weariness of familiarity. "You know what day it is. The review board is waiting."

"It's your anniversary?" Doc blinked in surprise.

"I wasn't paying attention to the date," Gideon said.

"Liar," Finch muttered while Milton visibly bristled.

"Still," Doc said, nodding to the guards, "best get on. I'll watch Elvis."

"And take a peek at my cards?" Gideon asked, if only to see how bristly Milton would get.

"I wouldn't dream—"

"That's enough, Doc," Milton snapped. "And you . . ." He grabbed Gideon by the collar. "On your feet, drone."

At which point Milton, who really hadn't been on the job long enough to know any better, found himself flat on the ground.

Finch, who had been on the job long enough to know better, snapped his shock stick to life while Elvis reared on his haunches. "You'll want to stand down, Quinn."

Gideon looked at Milton, whose red face now sort of matched the dirt, then he sighed, set down the cards, and dropped to his knees with his hands placed on his head. "Stay," he said to Elvis, and the draco relaxed onto all fours, hissing quietly.

"Guess that's the game," Doc said as yet more guards flowed from the inner gates.

"Dammit, Quinn." Finch shook his head at the prisoner while a cursing Milton struggled to his feet. "Are you *trying* to tank your chance at parole?"

"Grow up, Finch," Gideon said flatly. "They're never going to grant me parole."

"As of this day, February ninth, 1449 After Landing, it is the determination of this august board that Prisoner 66897, Gideon Quinn, be granted parole, effective immediately."

Gideon stared at that august board. "I have to say, I did not see that coming."

"*Quinn.*" Finch whispered the warning from Gideon's left.

It was twenty-some minutes after the kerfuffle in the yard, and Gideon was standing in front of the Honorable Warden Simkins, two members of the Corrections Board, and a ranking officer from the Corps.

And not just any officer, as General Kimo Satsuke had presided over Gideon's court-martial.

She hadn't changed much, he thought. Perhaps there were a few more lines accenting the sea-green eyes, and more silver shone in the black of her tightly braided hair than the day she'd sentenced him to life in the Morton Barrens.

Since Gideon had served only six years of that sentence, and was, to the best of his knowledge, still living, he found the sudden amnesty confusing, to say the least. "May I ask why?"

Finch made a small hiccuping sound.

"Ask the Corps," Warden Simkins replied, giving the general a glance.

Gideon turned his attention to Satsuke.

"It should be enough to know that your case has been reviewed and the sentence reduced to suit the discoveries," she told him.

Gideon felt his jaw tighten because it was absolutely *not* enough, and he opened his mouth to press for more detail when he caught Satsuke's stare.

The general possessed what could best be described as a very speaking gaze.

What her gaze was saying now was *shut your trap.*

He shut his trap, opening it only long enough for a terse, "Thank you."

"Don't thank me." Simkins slapped the folder in front of him closed. "I'd as soon see a traitor like you in the fields until crystal takes root in your eyes."

"I'll miss you too," Gideon said. Finch gave him a less than gentle nudge of the elbow, and Gideon added a belated, "sir."

Simkins was unimpressed. "The transport departs at twenty-one hundred hours. Dismissed."

Gideon found Doc waiting in his cell, keeping Elvis company and reading the chapters of *Curse of the Amazons* that Gideon had left in the pot.

"Odd, the board turning around your sentence like that," the older man observed. He was now leaning in the open door of the cell while Gideon changed into the clothes he'd last worn when he arrived in the Barrens.

Gideon, buttoning the trousers, which fit a bit loosely, swore he could hear Doc *not* ask the question, *Did you do it?*

Since Gideon had no intention of answering the unasked question, any more than he expected Doc to suddenly admit to having murdered his wife, he gestured to a matchstick reproduction of the Nikean Central Library sitting on the cell's lone shelf. "Do you want to keep that? I don't think it'll survive the trip."

"One of Nyal's," Doc murmured, studying the miniature work of art created by another inmate who'd been paroled some years earlier. "I'll put it in my office, and thanks."

While Doc fetched the sculpture, Gideon adjusted his suspenders and reached for the Infantry long coat.

But as he grabbed the coat, his gaze caught and held on the six names carved into the wall next to his bunk; a task that had taken most of his first year in the stir to complete.

Eitan Fehr, Estelle Carver, Bertie Walsingham, Anya Duvagne, Juster Siska, and Nbo Mulowa—half of Quinn's Dirty Dozen, immortalized in the dull stone of the Barrens.

As if he needed the reminder of who they'd been.

Or how they'd died.

CHAPTER 2

Nasa Territory
Treicember 21, 1442 After Landing

"Why is it so smogging hot in Treicember?"

The complaint, voiced by Corpsman Walsingham, filtered forward to where Gideon walked at the head of the company.

To Gideon's left, his sergeant, Nbo Mulowa shot a look his way, but neither chose to respond as both understood that, to Walsie, a day without bitching was like a day without sunsshine.

Instead, they continued to push through the whispering grasses of the savanna, which had that baked vegetation smell going, as the suns blazed overhead.

Squinting into the distance, Gideon adjusted the strap of his crysto-plas rifle, as it tended to chafe through the thin fabric of his shirt.

Walsie wasn't wrong. It *was* hot.

Hot enough that the entire company had stripped down to shirt sleeves, the iconic infantry long-coats rolled up and secured under their packs.

"How could it not be hot," Gideon heard Lieutenant Fehr reply to Walsingham's question with one of his own, "when we are so near the equator?"

Nbo snorted and Gideon's lip twitched.

Eitan Fehr, though as able a lieutenant as Gideon had seen, had only been with the company for a few months and hadn't yet mastered Walsie wrangling.

"Yeah, sir, I get that. But it's Treicember. That's *winter*," Walsie pointed out helpfully.

"Near the equator," Eitan echoed his earlier statement.

"And?" Walsingham asked.

"Do they not offer geography in Avonian schools?" the Fujian lieutenant asked in his turn.

"They might offer it, sir, but I sure didn't take it."

"And so much is made clear."

"Sir?"

"Nothing, Corpsman. Carry on."

Gideon smiled, then suppressed a curse as he almost walked into a pile of mammoth dung.

Nbo snorted again as Gideon sidestepped the mess, then almost tripped over a clump of sage from which a flurry of butterflies erupted.

A trumpeting rose from a herd of mammoths—possibly responsible for the mountain of dung he'd just bypassed—moving ponderously across the horizon.

Gideon looked over as Eitan came up on his right.

"Corpsman Walsingham was joking, was he not?" the lieutenant asked, resetting the sword he wore over one shoulder.

"I wouldn't count on it," Nbo said.

"Walsie's a basic soul," Gideon added.

"Is he at least aware Fortune orbits the suns?"

Gideon, Nbo, and Eitan all glanced back to where Walsie

was now walking alongside Anya Duvagne, once again trying to convince Anya that his rifle was superior to her crossbow for distance accuracy.

"I've never bothered to ask," Gideon replied as he turned forward. "I wouldn't worry, Lieutenant. Walsie may not be much for the big picture, but he can read a compass, field strip his rifle blindfolded, and smell a hostile two hundred meters off. He's basic," he repeated his earlier estimation, "but solid."

"He may be solid," Nbo commented as the voices from behind began to rise, "but if he doesn't stop needling Anya, she's going to punch him in the throat. Sirs." She nodded to both officers and turned back to put a stop to the bickering.

Gideon kept half an ear on the discussion, but he had zero doubts the sergeant would restore order, and in fact recognized her current tone as the same she used when wrangling her nine year old daughter.

Thinking of young Candace Mulowa, and the rest of Nbo's family, reminded Gideon the company was long overdue for a furlough. Fact was, they hadn't had more than a two day's break since before Eitan joined the twelfth.

He made a mental note to reach out to the brass once they'd completed the mission.

Who knew? If he timed it right, Dani's airship might also be back at Epsilon Base.

He glanced up as a talon of dracos soared overhead and wondered where the *Phalanx* was now.

"Do you not find it odd that General Rand seconded us to Spec Ops for this mission?" Eitan asked.

Shelving thoughts of Dani and furlough, Gideon looked at the other officer. "You've been with the company long enough to know odd is the twelfth's stock in trade."

"True," Eitan said before dropping his voice to add, "But

how often have your mission specs been delivered by a covert agent? Or included orders to burn after reading? And to be transported to a drop zone by a civilian 'ship?"

Gideon glanced at the lieutenant. "Did you get anything from the crew?"

"No, but they kept mostly to themselves," Eitan pointed out. "Which was also—odd."

"I'd agree," Gideon said, "but this is Special Operations we're talking about. The airship was probably one of theirs. Plus, the cypher on the orders was up to date, and given those orders involve meeting one of Spec Ops' exploring officers, I'd say some caution is warranted."

"But why would Special Operations not use one of their own teams?"

"My guess is they're worried about that dispatch we recovered in Fort Molina," Gideon replied before lowering his voice as well. "Orders to a spy embedded in the Corps likely set off a few swarms in Command."

"Yes, the mysterious Odile." Eitan murmured the code name of the dispatch's intended recipient. He let out a soft huff of breath, then angled his gaze toward Gideon. "Speaking of Fort Molina, have you heard from Msr Rand?"

At the question, the warm grass and sage odors surrounding Gideon were subsumed by the subtle, spicy memory of Celia Rand's perfume.

For a moment, he could again feel how she'd trembled against him, see her pulse jumping at her throat.

He swallowed as he again saw her lips parting slightly and her eyes, so wide and dark . . .

"No," he said, clearing his throat. "Why would I?"

Eitan's left brow arched. "You *were* injured on her behalf. That would typically merit at least a note of gratitude."

Gideon let out a huff of annoyance. "I was injured because she grabbed my arm in a panic. Anyway," He shrugged. "Msr Rand is yesterday's problem."

But even remembering that mission, and Celia, had him again thinking about Dani, and leave, and—

"And how is Lieutenant Solis?"

Gideon shot the younger man a look. "Are you reading me, Lieutenant?"

The dark eyes flicked to Gideon, then away. "No, sir," he said shortly. "That would be unethical, even if I could read another without physical contact."

"Sorry," Gideon held up a hand for peace. The last thing he needed to do was offend his 2IC. Especially since Eitan's being a sensitive had come in handy from time to time. "It could be I'm a little more stressed about this mission than I want to admit."

"So you do think it odd," Eitan prompted.

"Yeah," Gideon agreed with a sigh. "I do."

Eitan's lips quirked in an almost smile. "At least on this mission we have little chance of crashing an airship."

"It wasn't a crash. It was an aggressive landing."

"As you say."

Gideon caught the hint of humor but decided to let sleeping airships lie, and they continued in companionable silence until they reached the forested edge of the Nasa Escarpment, where they were to meet the exploring officer.

"Keepers," Eitan breathed as he looked over the edge of the cliff to the river valley far below.

"Smogging Earth on a stick." Walsie swallowed and eased away from the drop.

"Nbo," Gideon called back to his sergeant, "set up camp. No fires. Radio." He turned to find Estelle Carver, the radio operator, her dark face shining with perspiration as she shared a canteen with Corpsman Siska. "Set up your kit and listen for chatter. If there's enemy movement anywhere near this little slice of heaven, I want to know about it. Lieutenant," he turned to Eitan, "set the watch and make sure everyone knows the EO's password. Our man could be here at any time."

CHAPTER 3

By 2100 hours, Gideon had packed, completed his farewells, and staked out a spot in the prison's gate yard where three other parolees also waited.

The suns had long since set, taking the life-draining heat with them and leaving in its place a soul-sapping cold. Above the chill desert, the sky glimmered with optimistic stars, and a glow over the eastern wall presaged the imminent appearance of Ma'at, the first of Fortune's three moons to rise that night.

The other soon-to-be-ex-cons stood scattered about the holding area, overtly or covertly adjusting clothing not worn since the day of their arrival in the Barrens.

Clothing, Gideon noted, which now hung loosely on bodies pared down by years of labor in the crystal fields, giving the impression of a company of scarecrows awaiting field assignments.

Of the other scarecrows present, Gideon was only friendly with a grifter by the name of Horatio Alva.

The two had met when Gideon stepped between Horatio and a hard-timer named Pavel Escamilla, when the latter thought the former was "looking at him funny." The resulting throw-down had earned Gideon Horatio's undying gratitude, as well as a trip to the infirmary.

Horatio caught Gideon's roving gaze and gave him a nod and a quirk of a smile. Gideon returned the nod, but couldn't quite muster the smile.

He didn't know what it said that he felt more reassured by Horatio's impending freedom than his own.

"Is this all your kit?"

At the question Gideon turned, surprisingly unsurprised to discover General Satsuke at his side, apparently engrossed in the small pack on the ground.

"Didn't have much coming in."

Her eyes shifted from the pack at his feet to where Elvis crouched on Gideon's scarred pauldron, his tail twined around the twin suns of the Colonial Infantry tooled into the leather. "I don't imagine you had him coming in."

"I found Elvis a couple years ago," Gideon said, giving the draco a habitual tickle under the chin. "Elvis . . ." he gestured toward Satsuke. "Say hello to the general."

Elvis tilted his head up and bobbed it down long enough to make it seem a genuine bow before raising it up again with a low trilling sound.

Satsuke's brow rose slightly, then she nodded back to the draco before returning her attention to the draco's human. "You kept the coat," she observed.

"It's a good coat." Gideon shrugged, but gently because of Elvis. "And, I don't know if you've noticed, but it's balls-shriveling—it gets cold in the desert at night."

She favored him with a glare he felt certain was meant to mimic those desert nights. "I'd like a word in private."

She turned and strode towards an unoccupied corner of the gate yard and Gideon, after a beat, grabbed his pack and followed, noting the C.O.s spaced around the walls, should any of the parolees prove troublesome.

Gideon wasn't feeling troublesome; he was feeling curious. "So, I'm guessing it's you I have to thank for," he gestured to the gate, "all this?"

"Not me," she replied. "But it was my division that started the ball rolling."

Gideon said nothing, but the skepticism must have shown on his face.

"That surprises you?"

"I'm just trying to imagine a world where Special Operations gives a comb about an infantry colonel convicted of treason," he said, perversely pleased he could speak the word aloud and not choke on it.

"Normally we wouldn't," she agreed. "Especially when said colonel confessed." She shot him a pointed look. "But one of my officers was chasing a ghost . . ."

"Ghost?" he prompted, when she hesitated.

"Odile," she clarified.

Cold fingers ran up Gideon's spine at the name, but he kept his expression as blank as a really blank thing.

"Exactly." Satsuke sounded almost pleased as she responded to his silence. "A fool's errand, and one I refused to authorize."

At which point Gideon couldn't even pretend to hide his confusion. "Then why are you here?"

"I refused to authorize an investigation into Odile at the time of your conviction," Satsuke clarified. "But as time passed, it became clear there was still a hostile presence within the Corps."

"Presence?"

She grimaced, clearly unhappy. "Mission objectives leaked,

research facilities sabotaged, mobile units attacked with enough precision to tell us the enemy knew where they could be found. A steady stream of intelligence was being broadcast to the enemy up to the moment the Peace Accords were signed last Quaitember."

"Sorry, I can't take credit, this time." Gideon said, indicating the surrounding walls. "Been busy culling crystal for the past few years."

She gave him another of those "Night in the desert" glares. "Sarcasm doesn't become you."

"But it's so slimming."

"And I can see why your records include a disciplinary packet the size of a mammoth's leg."

"Misunderstandings, most of them." He shrugged again, this time causing Elvis to hiss. "Sorry," he said to the draco.

"Do you think we can at least attempt to stay on problem?" Satsuke asked.

"To be honest, I'm not sure what the problem is," Gideon countered. "The war is over. The good guys won, despite whatever ghosts you people think you have, so . . . why are you here? Why are we even having this conversation?"

"Perhaps I am here because, despite serving a brutal sentence for treason against the United Colonies, you still consider us the good guys," Satsuke told him and, while Gideon's breath caught, continued. "And not a little because, as my investigating officer pointed out, a man whose childhood home was destroyed by the Coalition, a man with over twelve years of service—a man who uncovered the existence of Odile in the first place—is unlikely to be guilty of treason, no matter what he confessed six years ago."

"Maybe that man was a lie," Gideon suggested, his voice oddly hollow.

"He might have been. In which case, I've just made a terrible mistake by arranging this parole. Were you aware," she added, "that General Rand has been given a position in the Corps Tactical Division in Nike City?"

Gideon wondered how she didn't get whiplash from the sudden change in topic. "They don't keep us apprised of Corps Command assignments down here," he managed.

"No," Satsuke murmured as the scrape of metal on stone indicated the opening of the main gate, "but unfortunately for you, Corps Command knows everything about your release, which means Rand will likely hear of it." A chime sounded, and Satsuke looked toward the gate. "It seems your transport is ready."

"All aboard!" the guard on the gate called out, and the other three parolees wasted no time lining up.

Gideon watched as the first stepped up to the guard to present the back of her right hand, on which her ident number had been tattooed.

Once the guard matched her ident number to the one on his list, she was allowed to pass through to the other side where, by law, she once again became a free citizen of the Colonies.

A free citizen with a permanent prison tattoo but, whatever.

"It's good you kept the coat," Satsuke said. He turned to see her watching him as she added, "This time of year can be quite cold in Nike City."

And Nike City, Gideon recalled, was where General Rand was stationed.

"66897!" Gideon's number echoed through the gate yard. "Quinn, you're up!"

"Here!" Gideon called out, but he was still looking at Satsuke. "Don't suppose you'd care to tell me the name of your investigating officer? The one who pushed for my release?"

"I don't suppose I would," she agreed, then nodded toward the gate. "Better get a move on."

Gideon held her gaze for another beat, then shouldered his gear and got a move on.

Once he cleared the gate, he spied the sleek military cutter Satsuke must have flown in on, then turned to climb the gangplank of the *Ramushku*, the prison's clunky supply freighter.

But as he reached the top of the *Ramushku*'s hatch, he shot one last look at the huddled shadows of the prison, where General Satsuke now stood in the open gate, watching him.

He couldn't make out her features, but he could see her fist rising to thump her heart in the Corps salute, which he returned, more out of instinct than intent.

But it was in that moment, as his tattooed fist struck his heart, that Gideon understood the truth; Satsuke might have released him from the Barrens, but until he uncovered the truth about Nasa, he would never be free.

CHAPTER 4

The first thing that struck Gideon was the water.

Not just that of the Avon River, flowing sluggishly a hundred meters from where Gideon stood, transfixed, on the *Ramushku*'s gangplank, but also the droplets of condensation sliding from the gondola to patter onto the tarmac, or hiss to vapor on the cooling engine pods.

There was even a mist rising from the river as the overcast sky darkened to twilight.

Moisture-heavy air filled his lungs and tickled his nose with a bright, mossy odor, before escaping again in the warm fog of his own breath.

Gideon wasn't a believer in the Old Earth concept of Heaven, but if such a place did exist, he wouldn't argue if it felt just like this.

Elvis was less entranced. The draco was crouched on his habitual perch on Gideon's right shoulder, tongue darting and triangular head tilting almost upside down as he tried to make sense of an atmosphere utterly unlike the desert of his hatching.

"You'll get used to it," Gideon murmured, still fixated by a landscape that didn't burn his eyes.

He could stand here forever, soaking in the damp.

"Anytime, mate," a gruff voice growled from behind.

Or he could get out of the way, which he did, before the aeronaut behind him escalated from gruff to surly.

Slinging his pack over his left shoulder, he cleared the steps and moved away from the *Ramushku*. "Well, Elvis, now what?"

Elvis gave a deep croon.

"Yeah, me neither." And so, at a loss, Gideon remained still, scratching his draco's head and staring out towards the city, ignoring the stares Elvis drew from passing airship crews and passengers. He hadn't been out of the world so long that he'd forgotten that domesticated dracos were a rarity.

Instead, he studied the deepening gray of the airfield, only stirring when a pair of aeronauts strode past.

"Smells like rain," one of the pair said.

"Rain? In Nike City?" her companion snorted as they angled towards the admin building. "Must be a day of the week."

But for Gideon, who hadn't experienced a drop of precipitation in six years, the mere mention of rain had him going weak at the knees.

Maybe there would be a downpour.

Maybe he could just lie down on the open airfield and bask in the sheer wetness of it all.

Or maybe that would be weird.

Probably it would.

He sighed and closed his eyes, trying to imagine how it would feel to be utterly drenched.

"All the cities in all the colonies and they decide to dump us in smoggin' Nike."

The declaration had Gideon turning to see Horatio Alva stopping at his side. "Didn't you have friends in the theatre here?" he asked, recalling Horatio's stories of the troupe he'd belonged to before the Barrens.

"The Rogues are a traveling company," Horatio explained before adding, "We were doin' a show in Nike when I got nicked."

"Ah," Gideon said.

"Yeah." Horatio huffed, still staring at the nearby city. "No swarming clue where the Rogues would be now. Or if they'd want—" He cut himself off.

"Sorry," Gideon said, knowing it was inadequate, and wondering, as he often had, what had driven the actor to grifting in the first place.

"No worries, mate," Horatio said with a shrug, the show of indifference belied by a flash of quiet yearning in his eyes. "Smog it," he cursed as the airfield lights flickered to life, their glow making the gray skies seem darker. "I'm for the river," he decided. "I'll lay odds that there's at least one steamer shipping out tonight." He glanced at Gideon. "Want to come along? Like as not one of them boats will be headin' to Ford."

"There's nothing for me in Ford," Gideon said.

Horatio nodded. "They say you can never find Earth again."

"Who'd want to?" Gideon wondered.

"True enough," Horatio agreed with a dry laugh before shouldering his pack. "Good luck to you, Quinn."

Because luck and I are on such good terms, Gideon thought. "You too," he said, but Horatio was already moving.

In moments, he was little more than one shadow amidst many, and soon lost to sight.

With a strange weight in his chest, Gideon turned his back on the river to find himself alone with the gently bobbing *Ramushku*.

The crew had long since dispersed, and there was no sign of the three other ex-cons who'd flown with them.

Focusing on the wet (Wet!) airfield, he considered his options because, unless he really wanted to bunk on the tarmac, he needed to get moving.

Except there remained the issue of which direction. He didn't know the city, had no local contacts, and was possessed of little more than a cranky draco and the short stack of starbucks granted each parolee.

Oh, and questions.

He had plenty of questions.

Those questions had him, for about the ten gazillionth time since the *Ramushku* raised anchor, chewing over Satsuke's intentions in setting him free.

Then, as he had the other ten gazillion times, Gideon reminded himself that Satsuke's intentions were none of his concern.

For now, and for the first time in a very long time, the only intentions that mattered were his.

All he needed to do was define said intentions, at the same time trying to adjust to living in a world with no guards, no Corps, no prospects . . . and no Dani.

Even as he thought this last, a woman stepped out from behind a stack of crates bearing the logo of Tenjin R&D.

"Gideon Quinn," the woman said. "We've been waiting for you."

Gideon took in the woman's simple clothing, the way her hand rested on the hilt of her crysto-plas shooter, and her stance.

He was also forced to admit, later and only to himself, he only registered the gun after he spent some quality milliseconds on her velvety brown face, green eyes, and prominent cheekbones.

"We?"' Gideon asked.

Even as he spoke, her partner appeared in Gideon's peripheral vision.

"We," she repeated.

"Ah," Gideon said, studying the newcomer, who was male, slightly taller than the woman, but with the same nondescript clothing, same coloring, same eyes.

A brother, Gideon assumed, and likely a twin.

Interesting.

Of greater interest was the weighted baton the he-twin held.

"You'll come with us," the she-twin said.

Gideon considered the statement. "Is that a request?"

"No." The he-twin raised his gleaming baton. "It's a fact."

"Uh huh," Gideon said, but rather than comply, he let out a short whistle and ducked left while Elvis launched to the right.

The he-twin lunged—too late—as the side-stepping Gideon grabbed his attacker's extended arm by the wrist, continuing to pivot and twist until the he-twin was forced to drop the baton, which bounced over the tarmac.

Elvis swooped down to claim the weapon in his hind claws, flapping off with it while Gideon swung the he-twin around to block the she-twin's shot.

Lucky for her brother, the she-twin pulled her shooter to one side in time for that shot to go high and wide, crackling in the open air and unnerving a pigeon roosting atop the stack of crates.

Gideon used the next half-second to bring the back of his fist to the brother's temple, stunning him before throwing him directly into the she-twin with enough force to knock her to the ground.

Joining the prone siblings, Gideon placed a careful boot on her wrist, applying just enough pressure for her to know he could apply more if she didn't release the shooter.

She released the shooter, and he kicked it across the tarmac.

"Backup?" he asked.

She grimaced. "Right boot."

Gideon nodded, checked the boot and, sure enough, found the knife she'd have thrown into him as he walked away.

He tossed the blade after the gun, checked the brother's boot, and found a—ha—twin to her own, took that and the short sword from he-twin's belt, and threw both in the opposite direction from his sister's.

Gideon looked down at the woman. "Tell General Rand I said hi."

Then he grabbed his pack, dropped during the skirmish, and clicked for Elvis.

Once the draco had come to land on Gideon's shoulder, he started toward the airfield gates to join the rest of the arriving passengers boarding the city-bound tram.

He looked up as a soft mist began to fall, muting the airfield's lights, and sheening the tarmac to a mirror finish.

It seemed that passing aeronaut had been right about the weather.

Perhaps it was the novelty of the rain, or the simmering haze of anger left by the fight, but when another figure slid from the shadows of the control tower to join the queue of inbound travelers, Gideon didn't notice.

CHAPTER 5

It wasn't until the tram had entered the city proper that Gideon remembered he had no idea where he was going.

All he knew of Nike was that it was the capital of the colony of Avon, that it housed the Tactical Division, and was home to the Shakespeare Circus.

Dani was, he recalled, very fond of the Circus, and had promised to take him if they could get a long enough furlough, but that was long ago, and they'd never made it to Nike.

Which was likely why, when the conductor announced their arrival in the ninth district, touting it as the home of Xanadu's, Marlowe Street, and the Shakespeare Circus, he chose to follow a number of other passengers off the tram.

The rest of the debarking travelers quickly scattered to parts unknown, though some spared a backward glance for Elvis, who was hunched on Gideon's shoulder, chittering at the rain. "Sorry," Gideon murmured to the draco as he looked around, then gave a soft "Yay," on spying a map tacked to the tram stop's kiosk.

Blinking away the rain, Gideon noted that, like his home

city of Turing, Nike followed the wheel plan, with all the government offices housed in the center of the wheel and twelve main avenues running from that center like spokes.

These spokes created eleven wedges of real estate which were, themselves, connected by streets which circumnavigated the city like variegated hoops.

"Oy, need a lift?"

Gideon and Elvis both started at the rickshaw driver's call. "No, thanks," he said, in part because he was mindful of the need to preserve his small amount of cash, and in part because he was not quite over the thrill of actual water falling from the sky.

The driver shook his hooded head and rode on, the wheels on his bike spraying Gideon's shins.

Gideon turned back to the kiosk map, where another moment's study revealed an inn that was not only less than a block from the Circus, it appeared to be operated by keepers. And while it always struck Gideon as odd how the defenders of the planet's wilds seemed to always insinuate themselves in human spaces, they could at least be depended upon to provide a clean bed and decent food, without being a drain on the pocket. He studied the map another moment before heading out into the downpour, an unhappy Elvis huddling close as he went.

"That one." Erasmus Ellison pointed at the man who'd just stepped from the airfield tram, looking somewhat lost.

Mia peered around her fagin's bulk to see who he meant.

Though Ellison's chosen mark was only on the other side of Lipton Street, she had to squint through the sheeting rain to see him. "Don't look rich," she said. But he did, to her experienced eye, look dangerous, even with that weird hump on his shoulder.

That comment earned her a clap on the side of the head that left her ears ringing. "Don't question, girl," Ellison snapped. "You're in enough of a stew, ain't ya?"

Mia hunched in on herself, which she'd long ago learned was the only safe response to Ellison when he was in a mood. And since he'd discovered her book cache only a few hours past, he was in a truly smogged mood.

"I told you time and again, readin' ain't nothing but a distraction," he said now, indicating he was still thinking about those books. "And dodgers lookin' for a distraction ain't challenged enough t'keep their head inna game, so *that*," he jerked his chin toward the tall man's apparent deformity, "is gonna be your challenge."

Looking closer, Mia was astonished to see the deformity move, stretching out first a head and then a pair of long, articulated wings.

"Oy!" she said, then before he could thump her again dropped her voice to whisper, *"He's got a draco!"*

"Not for long," Ellison said, glaring down, paying no mind to the rain sluicing from his bald head. "Once you nick it, it's gonna be *my* draco." He laid a hand on the girl's shoulder and gave it a squeeze she felt down to the bone. "You bring that winged bugger back to me, and it'll be double rations and a quarter the take once it's sold. If you don't bag it," he continued, leaning down so the rainwater dribbled from his head onto hers, "you'll be onna streets. You savvy?"

"Yeah—yes, sir," she amended, wincing as the heavy hand began to squeeze harder.

"Good. Now he's movin', so get on with ya', and remember," he added, "you don't bring me that draco, you'll be out of my hive."

He didn't add, because he'd long ago beaten it into every

one of his dodgers, how easy it was for a child to disappear in Nike.

What he *did* add was a slap on the back to start Mia on her way, nearly sending her face first into a muck-filled puddle. "And mind your feet," he hissed as though it were her clumsiness, and not his abuse, that had caused the misstep.

Gideon picked up the tail two blocks from the tram station.

A quick glance in a grocer's window told him his shadow was small and clad in the universal urban camouflage of patchwork trousers and hooded tunic he recalled from his own youth on the streets of Turing.

Six years ago, he might have given the dodger a shot at his wallet—a sort of paying-it-forward deal—but six years ago he'd possessed more than a scant handful of starbucks.

Since he didn't have enough to fill the kid's pockets, he opted for a detour through a narrow foot lane that bore a series of red lanterns. Here, among the gleaming ruby signs of a thriving night trade, Gideon figured his shadow would be tempted by the host of distracted, well-heeled marks seeking an evening's pleasure.

But even as Gideon wove through the crowds, avoiding umbrellas and propositions in equal measure, the dodger remained stubbornly fixed on him.

Weird, but since the kid was so determined, he decided to play along by winding through a few more detours.

And so did his shadow, who ignored the trove of pleasure seekers, and their wallets, just to keep up with him.

Maybe he should have taken a tour past a sweet shop or bakery, but, as time passed and the game continued, Gideon found he didn't mind the company.

In fact, the dodger was proving a pleasant distraction, as he was beginning to find the noise and bustle of the city somewhat oppressive.

Perhaps it was the crowds pushing around him that caused the niggling sense of displacement; or maybe it was the wanton flicker of business signs and streetlights after years of nothing but empty spaces and stars.

But the true cause of his discomfort didn't hit home until he stopped smack in the middle of crossing a street.

Not because of any oncoming traffic, but because, Gideon realized, he'd been subconsciously counting every step he'd taken since walking away from the tram station, and had reached 9,562.

For your average citizen, that number of steps would be a nice stretch of the legs and nothing more.

But for someone who'd lived in the Barrens, 9,562 steps was commonly considered to be the maximum number of steps an inmate could walk away from his work party and expect to get back alive.

So now Gideon stood in the middle of the street, fighting the habituated urge to turn back, if only because there was no *back* to go to.

He might have stood there indefinitely, but the chime of a rickshaw and a harried shout spurred him forward to the curb.

Once safe, he spent another damp moment quelling a bubbling resentment for the other people rushing, kvetching, laughing, or cursing their way through these rain-polished streets.

He resented them for not having to calculate how many mouthfuls of Morton kibble one could swallow before another inmate tried to steal your rations.

He resented them for not knowing how many sips of water one could afford to drink at once, because drinking it all now meant thirst later, but waiting risked loss to evaporation or theft.

Most of all, he hated them for never having to hesitate before taking that 9,563rd step.

It wasn't until he caught a hint of motion at the corner of his eye that he recalled the game of dodger vs. mark in play, and forced himself to continue, (being mindful to *not* count his steps).

This time he didn't stop until he turned onto Carroll Square, which consisted of a quartet of streets surrounding an agri-center. Each side of the square featured a mix of small businesses, eateries, and pubs, including the towering five stories of the Elysium Inn.

"What do you think," he murmured to Elvis, "do we keep our shadow following in the wet or settle in for the night?"

Elvis snorted and shook his head.

"Settle in it is," Gideon said and aimed for the inn. "There's the place," he said, loud enough for the would-be thief to hear, then added, this time to himself, "Hope they have private baths."

Elvis flapped his wings and crooned in what Gideon took to be agreement.

"There's the place."

As the tall fellow spoke, Mia pulled back into the nearest recessed doorway and waited for him to enter his chosen lodging.

She was relieved he'd finally stopped, especially after the disappointment of the district's red crystal alley, where she had expected him to seek out some company.

That would have provided her best chance at the draco, as

Mia had long since learned there were none so easy to rob as those in the throes of negotiated passion.

Then there'd been the point the fellow had stopped dead in the middle of Chaucer, where he came close to being flattened by an oncoming rickshaw.

She hadn't been able to stop herself calling out a warning, despite the fact that his untimely demise might give her a better shot at the draco.

Still, by the time he moved on, she'd come to conclude the man was a bit off in the head and figured she'd be doing the draco a favor by removing it from the suicidal maniac.

Now, as he at last entered the Elysium Inn, Mia held back, watching and waiting until, *honeycomb!* A light went on in a second floor window, street side.

Not as good as one of the alley-facing rooms, but better than those facing the pub on the other side, which would be busy well past fourteen midnight. But with the agri-center between the inn and the buildings on the opposite side of the square, anyone looking out a window would see nothing but trees, trellises, and rain-towers.

Plan already forming, she began to leave her shelter when movement on the other side of the street had her pulling back to watch another individual, dressed in clothes even darker than hers, moving from shadow to shadow before darting into the very alley Mia had been aiming for.

She eased back into the darkened stoop, wondering at the chances of someone else following the tall soldier.

Even as that thought struck, the someone else stopped in the light of a streetlamp and turned in her direction.

Though she could see no face, she did see, quite clearly, the hand which rose and pointed up to the newly lit room. After a measured pause, the hand dropped down, but the finger remained pointing straight up so Mia could easily see it shake back and forth in a distinct "no, no, no," fashion.

Then the hand fell, the figure turned and, in seconds, disappeared into the blackness of the alley.

Most people, faced with such specific opposition, would shrug and move on to the next mark. Then again, most people didn't have to deal with Fagin Ellison.

Oh no, you don't, Mia thought at her rival, already adjusting her plan of attack. *No one's getting that draco but me.*

How she meant to do that, she had no idea, but for starters, she moved from her current hiding space to the base of the agri-center's water tower, where she hunkered down to await developments.

As it happened, she didn't need to wait long because she'd barely slid under the shadows of the tower when her competition reappeared from the alley, no longer dressed entirely in black but sporting a new and wildly colorful ensemble.

Mia, certain she'd never before seen that particular shade of green, held her breath as the fellow paused at the alley entrance to scan the street, and let that breath out when, showing no signs of spying her, he turned and briskly entered the Elysium Inn.

Once he was safely inside, Mia dashed across the street and into the alley, where luck continued to be on her side as the inn's compost bin sat directly beneath the fire escape.

In a tick, she'd climbed the bin and was on the escape's lowest landing.

Another two ticks saw her climbing over the second-floor railing to the narrow ledge, barely half the width of her feet, and edging around to the room her mark had taken.

She could only hope she got to the draco before her quick-changing competitor.

CHAPTER 6

THE ELYSIUM HAD PRIVATE BATHS.

With an actual tub.

And doors that locked.

On the *inside*.

If this was a dream, Gideon hoped he never woke up.

He clicked at Elvis, who flapped over to perch on the edge of the sink, then let his dripping wet pack *splat* to the tile floor.

He stared a moment longer, then stepped back into the main room, furnished with the sort of sturdy, utilitarian furniture one might expect of keepers. But while the furniture was plain, the bedding was soft and rich with autumn colors, the wheat-gold walls draped with tapestries, and the bamboo floor cushioned by a Fujian rug.

It was, to Gideon's sensory-deprived diet, a veritable banquet of textures.

The room also featured a meditation nook should the traveler wish to indulge, but Gideon doubted he'd make use of the space.

Dani had enjoyed meditation, but Gideon figured a person who regularly jumped out of airships with nothing but a slender tether between herself and a fatal splat would need to maintain a certain level of chill.

Studying the nook, he wondered if she still meditated.

Or if she was still in the Corps.

Or even still alive.

"Stop it," he said aloud, forcing his thoughts away from the woman he'd lost—*not lost, sent away*, he reminded himself—and toward something more productive.

Because if he was going to think about anyone, it should be Jessup Rand and the two mercenaries Rand had set on him the second he set foot in Nike, or the dodger who'd trailed him to the inn.

Or, he said to himself as he turned to look at the bathroom, *you could not think of anyone at all.*

And for once, Gideon thought his self might have a point.

For this one night, he could just enjoy the moment and this room. This clean, private, empty—

The sound of a fist on wood broke into his determined revery, reminding Gideon he'd asked the keeper at the desk to have dinner delivered to his room.

He opened the door with caution but found only another keeper, this one young and slightly flushed and, most importantly, carrying a tray crowded with steaming dishes.

Gideon could have kissed him, but as they'd not even been introduced, he restrained himself.

Taking custody of the tray, he thanked the keeper politely, then closed and latched the door, then turned to face the room and froze, suddenly indecisive.

The scents rising from the tray—which held a bowl of soup, some warm naan, a plate of lentil stew, and skewers of roast aurochs—were reducing him near to tears.

But then there was that bathtub, begging to be filled.

He looked at the tray, then at the bathroom door, then back at the tray.

Several minutes later, Gideon eased into a tub filled with steaming hot water.

The tray sat on the floor, within easy reach of hungry bathers.

He could only hope whoever was following him had been a dodger, willing to move on to another target. Or, if it was one of Rand's operatives shadowing him, that they would do the sensible thing and wait until he turned out the lights to try anything stupid, because if anyone dared interrupt him now, Gideon would happily kill them.

In the corridor outside Gideon's room Bren, the young keeper who'd delivered his meal, spared a moment of gratitude that the guest hadn't commented on the soup bowl being not as full as it ought, thanks to the guest in the bright green jacket.

The man hadn't been watching where he was going and walked right into Bren's elbow, upsetting the soup.

At least the fellow had helped to mop up the mess, mostly by fluttering his handkerchief about so much it was a miracle nothing else spilled.

Clumsy fellow, Bren thought as he headed for the stairs, and no taste in clothing, but decent enough.

While Bren whistled his way down the back stairs to his station, Nahmin Soor tugged the memorable bright green jacket into place and headed down the front stairs.

Dosing the soup in transit had been a calculated risk, but

since Quinn chose to eat in the privacy of his room, some creativity was required.

At least Nahmin had seen the full dose make it into the soup, which meant, assuming Quinn was hungry, he'd be ready to collect within the hour.

Plenty of time to call for the carriage.

Still, as he made his way through the lobby, Nahmin couldn't shake the sensation that, by leaving the target still breathing, he was in some way cheating.

This, Gideon decided, could well be the ultimate dining experience.

Lounging in a tub filled with steaming water, he was currently using the last bit of naan to mop up every drop of sauce from the lentil stew.

He'd already done justice to the soup and one of the skewers of aurochs, while Elvis put paid to the second.

Only the bowl holding a piece of laden honeycomb remained untouched.

A cup of tea, poured from the squat teapot included with dinner, sat on the tub's ledge, adding its own modest trail of steam to that of the bathwater.

On the edge of the sink, Elvis was grooming himself after neatly dispatching his share of the aurochs, easing Gideon's concerns that the draco would prove resistant to food that didn't squeak prior to being devoured.

All in all, the draco seemed to be adjusting nicely.

And if the warm, sleepy glow infusing his body was any indication, so was Gideon.

With a satisfied sigh, he set the clean plate alongside the rest of the empty dishes, contemplated the honey and decided to hold off, content for the moment with the tea, of which he managed one or two sips before his muscles began to melt into the warm water.

Going with it, Gideon set the cup aside, let his head rest against the back of the tub, and soaked in the tangible proof of his freedom: food (not a dehydrated, rehydrated food-like substance but actual food); un-rationed water; and a door that closed with—and again, this could not be overstated—a lock on the *inside*.

It was close to perfect.

Certainly closer than he'd any right to expect.

Lounging, eyes closed, in water up past his chest, he could only assume events of an unpleasant nature would soon infringe on the near perfection, and then life would once again revert to its unpleasant norm.

Cynic, a voice from his past chided him.

Realist, he corrected the memory before sliding easily into the dream.

"Of course. Forgive me, how could I forget your motto?" the memory said, standing at the side of the tub, studying him. "How did it go? 'Don't get comfortable, don't even make dinner plans because if you do, life will just serve you up a dish of pain.'" She leaned over and traced one of several scars over his ribs. "You've tasted more than your share."

"Dani . . ." Her name came out as little more than a breath, stirring the water.

"Were you expecting someone else?" She sat on the edge of the tub, seemingly unconcerned that her uniform was getting wet.

"I wasn't expecting anyone at all."

She danced her fingers over the water, head tilting as she met his gaze. "Why are you looking at me that way?"

"Because you're not real."

"True," she said with a small, sad smile.

Mia, squinting through the rain, had just come even with her target's room when a motion below prompted her to flatten herself against the slick granite.

Peering down, she saw the man in the garish green coat and yellow pagri making a beeline out of the inn, heading to the corner of Carroll Square.

Did that mean he'd already gotten to the draco?

She focused on the retreating back to confirm there was no sign of a pouch or box, no suspicious lumps, just the bright slim figure of a man in a hurry to be some place else.

Which meant either he'd been unable to get hold of the creature or the draco wasn't his goal.

But what did the raggedy man have to take, if not the draco?

As she asked the question, she heard a small crash, like a bit of crockery breaking, from inside the nearest window, drawing her closer. Easing forward, she cautiously peered through the fogged pane and into what turned out to be a brightly lit bathroom, where she got her first truly good look at the object of her fagin's desire.

The draco was perched at the edge of the sink, rearing up on his hind legs, and he was brilliant, with his iridescent brown-gold scales and bright eyes. Mia's breath caught in her throat, and for a moment she forgot she was standing on a narrow ledge in the rain with her fingers and toes going numb with the cold of it.

Only for a moment, however, and since there appeared to be no one else in the room, she angled for a better view of the draco, whose neck and wings were now outspread. He was so close she could even see his pupils, thinned to mere slits as his head turned to the bathtub.

So intense was his focus on that particular feature, Mia couldn't help but follow the draco's single-minded gaze.

The first thing she spied was the broken teacup on the floor. Then her eyes moved further left, and she saw the tub, the water sloshing over the edge, and lastly the draco's owner sliding, all unaware, under the surface of the steaming bathwater.

Her smile had always undone him.

"I missed you," Gideon said.

"Then why did you send me away?"

"It's—complicated," he said.

"That was a pathetic answer six years ago," she chided gently, "and it hasn't improved with age."

"Does anything improve with age?"

"Wine, Infantry long coats," she glanced at his, where it lay folded neatly on the floor, "'Blue Suede Shoes'—the song, not the footwear—and us," she said lastly, no longer smiling. "We could have improved with age, if you'd given it half a chance."

"There was no chance." He wondered how it was possible for a dream to hurt so deeply. "Not after Nasa."

"And yet here you are, holding on to a dream."

She wasn't wrong. And not only because, without thinking, he'd taken hold of her hand.

Carefully, he released it.

"Gideon," she murmured.

In reproof?

In forgiveness?

He would never know because, though she'd been his for a brief, bright once upon a time, life had indeed served up a dish of pain. And Gideon, refusing to let Dani share that particular dish, had pushed her away.

She'd pushed back—hard—but in the end, his stubbornness proved greater than hers.

"Gideon."

He blinked, looked up to see she was studying him with an expression he could only hope wasn't pity.

"You need to wake up now." She placed the hand he'd released to his cheek.

"If I wake up, you'll leave."

"I was never here," she reminded him, then placed her lips, warm and silky as the bathwater, over his. "Wake—"

"—up already, won't you?" Mia didn't know how many times she'd shouted at the man since dragging his head out of the water. Her arms were already trembling as she tried to keep him from sliding down again. Though she'd pulled the plug first thing, the water was draining too bloody slow, so she just kept holding on and yelling and hoping she wasn't shaking a dead man.

Not that he felt dead.

Not that she knew what dead felt like.

From the way the draco was acting, shifting from leg to leg to leg to leg on the tub's ledge and crooning anxiously, she wasn't the only one.

"He'll be all right," she told the frenetic beast, then turned her attention back to the inert head on her shoulder. "You better be all right," she said, giving him a massive shake and a thud on the chest, which she vaguely remembered seeing a riverman do to one of his mates who'd been pulled from the water after too long a spell.

When did Dani's voice get so high? And why is she hitting me?

Gideon opened his mouth to ask just that when a mouthful of brackish water erupted from his lungs, and he coughed so violently, he fell over on his right side.

"No, no! Not that way!" The voice that wasn't Dani's bounced around his ears.

"What way?" he asked, or rather, tried to ask. What came out was more a wet gurgle as he inhaled a mouthful of water.

He thought he heard a "No, no, no, no," but everything was muffled.

Then a deep and tearing pain dug into his left shoulder, shredding the fog shrouding his thoughts and galvanizing his body into action.

Jerking out of the wet, and with the aid of a pair of fairly determined hands, he got himself sitting up enough to cough out the water he'd sucked in while not-Dani thumped him vigorously on the back.

"Bleeding beehives!" Not-Dani ceased the thumping as his eyes opened, then she began to curse like an infantry drill sergeant.

Gideon appreciated the sentiment, and would have echoed it, but at the moment he was still working on basic respiration.

He did manage to lift his head enough to see his savior, but closed his eyes again because it appeared there were three smallish, somewhat hazy people in front of the tub, along with an entire talon of dracos flying from one end of the bathroom to the other.

Which meant that, as predicted, life had indeed reverted back to unpleasantly normal.

CHAPTER 7

The small person—girl, Gideon's slowly focusing mind told him—drove away the last whispers of the dream, though her voice still sounded muffled, like it came to him through a lake.

Or fog.

Gideon had experienced such a fog more times than he cared to count, in an assortment of medical facilities.

"Msr?" the girl asked again.

Gideon held up a "just a minute" finger or three, then leaned over the bathtub's edge and shoved said finger(s?) down his throat until he could successfully puke up what had been mostly a very nice dinner, with the small exception of the morph included somewhere in the meal.

"Oy! That's disgusting."

"I couldn't agree more," he croaked, flopping back into the tub.

The girl's head tilted inside the hood of her tunic. "Then why'd you do it?"

"Because unless you're under the surgeon's knife, morpheus is better out than in."

"And how d'ye know . . ." she began, then stopped herself. "Because you've been under a surgeon's knife."

"A time or three." He reached out and grabbed the towel draped over the edge of the bathtub. Once he'd covered as much as possible, he leaned back again and closed his eyes, because seeing was still an unpleasant proposition.

"You gonna die?"

He raised an eyebrow but didn't open the eye. "Not presently, I don't think."

A moment of expectant silence passed, but what the kid expected he couldn't say.

He also couldn't say why there was a kid in the bathroom in the first place, or why a stiff, cold breeze shivered over his skin, or why he heard the steady sound of rain.

He should probably ask about that.

He didn't, not even when he heard the sound of water running from the sink's tap or felt a hot, damp cloth pressed to the talon marks on his shoulder.

Talon.

Draco.

Elvis!

If the window was open . . .

But then he felt the distinctive touch of the draco's head against his cheek and relaxed.

"He sure likes you," the girl said.

"We've been through a lot together."

"Looks like you've been through more," she observed. "I ain't never seen so many scars."

He thought she shouldn't be seeing them now, except it wasn't that big a towel.

"How'd you get so messed up?" she asked.

A childhood in occupied Turing, half a lifetime soldiering, six years in hell, he thought.

"It's complicated," he said to the backs of his eyelids.

This statement was met with another silence, followed by more running water, followed by the slopping, scraping, swooshing sounds of someone cleaning up.

He cracked an eye open to see the girl using the last clean towel to dump the broken shards of his teacup in the waste bin before moving over to the—aha!—busted window to clean up those shards.

At least now he knew why it was so cold.

He looked over the side of the tub and noted she'd used the second-to-last clean towel to wipe away his regurgitated dinner. He didn't ask where said towel had ended up.

"Who on toxic Earth would ruin a nice dinner with enough morph to knock out a mammoth?" he asked instead.

"Someone what wants you dead?" The girl shoveled window glass into the bin.

"Guess that rules you out," he commented. "By the way, I'm Gideon. Thanks for saving my life."

She shrugged, but rather than offer her own name, dropped the glass-filled towel into the bin with a shake of her hand, sowing the bright white fabric with a field of tiny red drops.

"You're bleeding." Alarmed, Gideon tried to stand and instantly regretted the attempt, not just because of the lingering dizziness but because he almost dropped the towel.

That earned a snort from his damsel to the rescue. "So are you." She pointed to the cloth on his shoulder, stained with long red streaks.

"Still, you should clean that hand."

"Already did, mother, but thanks." Though she did take a moment to pat it dry with a bit of tissue, but only, Gideon felt certain, to keep him from fussing.

"How'd you cut yourself, anyway?" he asked, then answered his own question. "You cut yourself when you broke the window. But why did you break the window? *Right,* because you were outside," he continued the trend.

She stared. "You talk to yourself a lot, then?"

He stared back. "You were *outside?*"

"Well, I wasn't hiding in the loo, was I?"

"Okay. But . . . why?"

"Would you rather I left you to drown?"

"Absolutely not. But you know, most folks would wonder why a kid your age would even be in the position to break a second-story window so she might come to the assistance of a drowning man in the first place. Then again, I'm not most folks, and neither are you, I'm guessing. Just like I'm guessing you're the one who started tailing me at the tram station."

He enjoyed a brief flash of triumph in being able to surprise the seemingly unflappable girl.

The enjoyment was quickly squashed as she shoved a loose coil of black hair behind her right ear. The sleeve of her tunic fell back, revealing the livid bruise around her wrist.

That got him to his feet.

"Who did that to you?"

"What? Who did what?" She looked around herself, startled.

"That stinger of a bruise you're sporting," he said, one hand on the wall and the other gripping the towel firmly in place.

"It ain't nothing," she said, yanking her sleeve down.

"Isn't anything," he corrected automatically and almost laughed at the look she shot him. "Sorry, but seriously, did your fagin do that?"

She bit her lip, then shrugged. "What would you know about fagins?"

"Only what I learned from mine, back in the day."

"Your . . . *you* had a fagin?" That got her interest. "Nah."

She dismissed the idea immediately. "No way you was a dodger."

His head tilted as he considered the kid. "Why not?"

"Because," she said with the air of one pointing out the obvious, "you're old."

"Well, ouch."

"I mean, you know, you're grown up, is all."

"I didn't start that way."

"Fine," she shrugged again, "but not many who start as dodgers sign on to the Corps, do they?"

"They did if they were dodging during the Turing occupation," Gideon countered, then frowned as he habitually avoided reminiscing over his days in Turing.

"You were dodging during the occupation?" the girl echoed, clearly impressed. "You're even older than I thought."

This time Gideon did laugh, but the laugh was wet and turned to a cough, and Elvis, disturbed by his person's distress, crawled along the edge of the tub to press his head against Gideon's leg.

"Good boy," Gideon said. "It's okay, you did okay." He'd be feeling the slices from Elvis's talons for a month, but it beat drowning.

He glanced up, saw the girl watching their interaction.

"So, one dodger to another, why did you target me? I mean, it's kind of obvious I'm not rolling in starbucks."

The girl didn't answer, but her eyes darted to Elvis, then to the floor.

"You wanted Elvis," Gideon realized. "You wanted my draco." He thought about that. "Why did you want my draco?"

"Not me," she said quickly. "Fagin Ellison's the one who wants it, and he only wants it because ain't no one else in Nike has one, they're that rare."

"And rare means pricey," Gideon said, quietly furious with

himself for not giving a second thought to traipsing the streets of a crowded city with Elvis perched on his shoulder.

The smart thing would have been to let Elvis take flight and tail Gideon to the inn.

Of course, had he done that, there would have been no dodger at the bathroom window when the morph took effect and he wouldn't be standing here, in a tub, with a towel wrapped around his middle, making himself dizzy playing what-if.

He looked at the girl, who was watching him, balanced forward on the balls of her feet, ready to run.

"Tell me about Ellison," he said.

"Naught to tell," she said, looking away.

"Okay," he said as, with some care, he stepped out of the tub. "Let's start with you don't have to worry about me calling the filth. After all this?" He indicated the tub where he'd likely have drowned without her help. "There's no way I'd swear a complaint. I also won't let you go back empty-handed, but your fagin's going to have to make do with whatever cash I can spare, because taking Elvis is not an option."

"But then I'll be out!" she protested in a voice sharpened by fear. "That's what he said when he marked you. To come back with the draco or not at all. If I don't bring Elv—that draco—then I'm as good as dead."

"That's not—"

"Not gonna happen? Is that what you think?" She lifted her chin, all youth and defiance. "Maybe you was a dodger, maybe you wasn't, but you ain't one of Ellison's—"

"Aren't," Gideon murmured.

"—hive," she continued over his grammatical distress. "Ain't a dodger in Nike ever left Ellison's protection and lived to tell it."

"It's not supposed to work that way." Even as he said it, Gideon knew it was an asinine statement because obviously—

"That's how it is," she confirmed his thoughts with a weary certainty. "I do what he says, or I'm done." She gave Elvis, peeking from behind Gideon's leg, another look. "Guess I'm done."

"No, you're not. I won't let that happen." From her expression, he figured his promise sounded as asinine as his previous statement. "I know there's no reason to trust me—"

She snorted, he presumed in agreement.

"—but you're going to have to trust me. Mostly because, even if I were willing to let him go, Elvis wouldn't leave me. You've seen what he can do when he's motivated." He pulled the damp cloth from his shoulder to display the evidence. "And he *likes* me."

Something in her eyes told him she thought it might be worth the risk. Or maybe she'd just like to see Elvis have a go at her fagin. Either way, there was still something he didn't understand, and he found he needed to. "If you're so sure this Ellison will put you out, why didn't you just leave me to drown?"

She shrugged, scuffed her feet. "I may be a dodger, but I sure as comb ain't no killer."

A distinction Gideon could appreciate, but it also got him thinking. "I'm not sure whoever dosed the soup was either. Morpheus is a sedative, not a poison."

"And?" she asked, then slapped herself on the forehead. "And no way the fop would know you'd be nutter enough to eat your dinner inna tub!"

"Yes. Not exactly how I'd put it, but yes. Wait," he held up his hand. "What fop? Do you know who dosed me?"

"I don't *know*, know. I just seen this bloke leaving while I was out there." She pointed to the window. "Poison-green jacket and yellow trousers. Couldn't miss 'im."

"And his fashion sense makes you think he did it?"

"No." She huffed, he presumed at the idiocy of adults. "I think he done it—"

"Did it," Gideon corrected automatically.

"—because *he* was following you too."

"Huh," Gideon managed. For a guy less than two days out of prison, he was proving awfully popular.

"Bugger tried to warn me off'a you too," the girl continued, then went on to describe her rival's actions, from the way he'd changed his clothes in the alley before entering the inn's front door, to his departure just as she'd reached Gideon's window. "I wasn't planning on coming in so soon," she admitted, glancing at Elvis, then the tub. "But then I did."

"Okay," Gideon said. Then he tilted his head. "Are you hungry? Because I'm hungry."

Her mouth actually dropped in surprise. "Didn't you just eat?"

"Temporarily." They both looked at the trash bin. "Besides, whoever dosed me might be coming back." As he spoke, he stepped around the girl to where his clothing lay, by now partially dry.

"But whoever dosed you would be thinking you're out cold. Why not stay here and, you know . . ." She punched a fist into her hand as she added, "Give 'em a good pounding for their trouble?"

"Because as much as I'd enjoy it, I'm not in full pounding form just now." He reached down to pick up his trousers, and as if to prove his point overreached, missed the trousers, and almost fell over.

She sighed, loudly, then grabbed a handful of clothing and thrust it at him.

"Thanks." He took the clothes, straightened up, and waited.

She crossed her arms over her chest and waited too.

"Do you mind?" he asked, making a "turn around" gesture.

"Mind what?" The girl looked confused, then the crystal flared. "Ohhh." She drew the word out into three syllables, then grinned. "Fordians are so priggish. Ain't you never been to the Fujian baths?"

"Often enough to know even they have age restrictions. How old are you anyway? Eleven?"

"Thirteen," the girl responded, unoffended. "Best guess, any road." Still, in deference to what she obviously considered unnecessary modesty, she did turn around to stare out the window where, Gideon noted, the rain had finally ceased.

Ignoring the semi-damp garments, he dressed quickly, hands still shaking somewhat as they buttoned up the trousers. He ditched the padding over his shoulder before donning his shirt—it wasn't the first time he'd gotten blood on his clothes.

By the time he got to the boots, he could tell right from left, which was nice, and soon he was sliding his arms into his coat and clicking for Elvis.

The girl turned in time to see the draco land on his right shoulder. "So," she said, "where we going?"

He was encouraged by the *we*. "Don't have a clue. Got any suggestions?"

She considered him, then seemed to come to a decision. "I know a place, nothing too posh, mind, down on Marlow—*oy!*" The street name turned into a squeak as Elvis leaped from Gideon's shoulder, wings brushing the girl's hood on the down-sweep.

In one flap, he was at the windowsill, where he scented the air briefly before turning his eyes downward and letting out a low keen that was the draco equivalent of a canine's warning growl.

"Keepers!" the girl said, obviously impressed.

Gideon said nothing but moved to the window himself,

where he stood carefully to the side so anyone looking up wouldn't see him. "Ah," he said. "Of course."

"What?" The girl joined him, trying to peer around the tall man and the draco. "Of course what?"

"That." He nodded toward the coach and four pulling into the square.

That there was a horse-drawn carriage at all was impressive, as most city dwellers used public transpo. The moderately well-off might spring for a crystal-batt car or cycle, but only ristos had enough of the ready to support livestock that had no purpose other than to look good.

More impressive still, the four horses drawing the carriage were perfectly matched blacks, and the carriage itself was big enough to hold six comfortably, eight if you weren't prudish.

"Nice," the girl said, standing on her toes to better see the vehicle, "if you're into that sort of thing."

"They are." Gideon nodded toward the family crest emblazoned on the glossy black door. "That's the Rand family crest."

"So what does that mean?"

"It means," he said as the horses rounded the square to pull up at the lodging's entrance, "it's time to find the back door."

CHAPTER 8

THEY FOUND THE BACK DOOR BY THE SIMPLE ACT OF looking for the kitchen, which Mia, and every dodger worth their honey, knew was the emergency exit of choice for those in need of a quick departure.

Given the staff didn't blink an eye as a soldier, a dodger, and a draco burst in to weave through the steaming pots and clashing dishes of dinner prep, Mia had to assume they were used to the occasional emergency exit.

One young fellow did look up long enough to ask Gideon how his dinner had been.

"Better going down than coming back up," Gideon said.

Mia snorted, then dashed past Gideon as he paused to request his room be held for the time being, but the soldier was right quick, slipping round front of her so he was first to ease out the alley door, which opened right next to the compost bin she'd used to climb up to Gideon's floor.

She almost commented on it when Gideon came to a sudden halt, hissing a curse.

Mia took it as a warning and, rather than step into the open, used Gideon as cover as she slid to the right, tucking herself between the wall and the odiferous compost bin in time to hear a woman say, "If you or the draco so much as twitch, I will kill it."

"Understood," Gideon replied without hesitation.

Whoever this woman was, Mia figured she was trouble.

"I have to say," the woman continued, "I am surprised to see you standing upright. We were expecting you to be sound asleep in your room. Nahmin must have gone light on the morph."

Nahmin, Mia thought, *that must be the ponce.*

"Nahmin's dosing wasn't off," Gideon said. "It knocked me pretty well out. Almost drowned me, in fact."

"That would have been a shame," the woman said.

Mia didn't think she meant it.

"I'm not sure you mean that." Gideon seemed to agree.

"But I do," the woman insisted. "You and I, we have unfinished business."

"We do? Oh, you mean because of the thing back at the airfield."

Mia almost snickered at Gideon's exaggerated tone. Was he *trying* to make the woman mad?

"Yes," the woman replied, sounding pretty mad, "because of the . . . thing."

"How is your brother, anyway? He is your brother, right?"

"My twin, Ronan," she said. "And I am Rey."

"Gideon Quinn, but you knew that. So, where is Ronan-your-twin?" Gideon continued in a "we're just mates catching up on old times" fashion.

"Recovered enough to seek you in your rooms."

"I'm glad to hear it," Gideon said.

"I'm not sure you mean that," she echoed his earlier opinion.

"Seems to be a lot of that going around."

Odd, how Mia could hear the man's smile.

"You know what else is going around?" the woman asked, and Mia now heard the distinctive hum of a crystal shooter warming up.

"An appalling lack of composting in the inner city?" Gideon asked.

Mia rolled her eyes because, even if Gideon wasn't facing an angry woman with a live weapon, it was a silly statement to make. Keeper waste bins were the crystal standard of composting, so why—

"No," the woman said, apparently in response to Gideon's suggestion. "What is going around lately, is pain."

Which was when Mia, who understood Gideon even better than she herself knew, put her shoulder to the corner of the compost bin and her feet to the wall and *pushed*.

Gideon, still staring down the barrel of a live shooter, wasn't sure the dodger had gotten his hint until he heard the telltale groan of the compost bin's wheels.

She got the hint! he thought, as Rey instinctively turned her weapon towards the new threat, allowing Gideon to dart behind the massive bin as it rolled forward, creating a blockade between himself and the mercenary.

Wheels squeaked, Elvis chittered, and brick and metal shrieked as the corner of the bin gouged the wall on the other side of the alley.

"You got the hint," he said as the dodger joined him.

"Yeah, yeah, I got the hint. Now can we scarper?"

From behind the wall of compost, they could hear Rey's curses, interspersed with the occasional blast from her shooter.

"You bet," he said, making sure the dodger remained ahead of him and Elvis secure as they made their escape.

"How'd you know the composter was wide enough to block the alley?" she asked as they turned onto the street behind the hotel.

"I didn't." Gideon shrugged at her expression of affront. "I figured it'd be enough to have a mammoth-sized compost bin bearing down on her. The blockade was just luck."

"You're a right nutter, you are."

"So I've heard." Gideon glanced around. "They'll be past that bin soon enough. We have to get out of sight."

"That way." The girl pointed to a brightly lit pleasure emporium on the other side of the street.

Gideon didn't have to read the sign blazing over the arched entrance to recognize Dani's beloved Shakespeare Circus, Nike's sprawling ode to the dramatics.

Dani had told him how the Circus stages—all housed under one roof—varied in size and shape, from intimate cabarets for twenty to auditoriums which held two hundred. And such was the Circus's popularity that tonight, despite the weather, the place was hopping.

Even now a small horde converged on the stage nearest the open gates, where a placard announced a performance of *A Comedy of Errors*.

"It's a sign," Gideon said, indicating the placard.

"Yeah, I can see it's a sign," the dodger replied. "I ain't blind."

"No, I meant because it's the *Comedy of Errors* and tonight's sort of a—forget it."

"Right."

But as they neared the main gate, Gideon thought of crowds, and dracos, and Mia's fagin, and then he clicked twice and said, "High road."

Elvis, hissing, leaped from his roost on Gideon's pauldron

and flew to the peak of the Circus roof, where he'd be wet and grumpy, but also safe.

At a tea stall not far from the stage where *A Comedy of Errors* was about to begin its second act, Mia's heavy-handed fagin sat nursing a cup and keeping a weather eye on two of his dips.

As it was a busy night, and Ellison expected a good haul, he'd just splashed a celebratory dose of whiskey into his steaming cup when he spied the tall soldier he'd set Mia on over two hours past.

The man was moving quickly through the crowds, eyes everywhere, as if searching for something.

He was also without his draco, which Ellison took to mean Mia had succeeded in the challenge of stealing the beast.

Already counting the starbucks the draco would bring, he toasted the departing soldier and took a hefty sip.

Then the masses parted and he saw Mia on the far side of the soldier, walking *with* him—with nary a draco in sight—and the spit take which followed this discovery struck one half of a set of twins walking past.

By the time he was able to placate the angry pair, Ellison had lost sight of Mia and could only stalk in the direction of his wayward dodger, while the fuming twins stormed in the opposite direction.

A little over an hour later, Gideon followed the girl off his second tram of the evening and down Marlowe Street, while Elvis kept pace overhead.

"Why are you counting?" she asked.

Gideon, who'd just reached twenty-three, grimaced. "No reason." He gestured for her to continue.

A silent seventy-two steps later, they arrived at Kit's Diner.

Elvis came to rest on the diner's awning while Gideon scanned the street, but other than a few happy souls exiting a nearby pub bearing the name Here's One in Your Eye, Marlowe Street was quiet.

While the girl opened the door, Gideon looked at Elvis. "You'd better stay out here."

Elvis chittered his displeasure at that idea.

"It's for your own safety," Gideon said.

Elvis glared down, seemingly unconvinced.

"Fine, I'll bring you a little draco bag," Gideon promised, then followed his young guide into the diner, where the warm air was redolent of oats, cinnamon, butter, and the sharp slash of bacon.

His mouth commenced watering even as his eyes skimmed the small space, which had five booths running along the left-hand wall, a handful of four tops in the middle, and a counter fronted by well-worn, red-cushioned stools on the right.

The kitchen was open to the dining area via a long pass-through, though he couldn't see anyone inside the kitchen. Only one of the booths was occupied, by a young man with mussed gold-brown hair, wearing a UCAS Air Corps jacket that had seen better days.

The aeronaut looked up, and Gideon watched him acknowledge his own Infantry coat, which had also seen better days.

The two shared a brief look, a short nod, and then the younger man's brown eyes returned to the cup of tea he was nursing. There was an empty plate in front of him, all but licked clean, which gave Gideon a certain optimism about the fare.

A kettle began to whistle, and Gideon turned toward the

sound in time to see a young woman with burnished copper hair appear through the open arch between the kitchen and counter area, carrying a stack of clean plates.

Not only young, Gideon noted as she made for the steaming kettle, but pregnant.

Upon spying new customers at the door, she assayed a tired smile, one that became genuine the moment they fell on the girl at his side.

"Honey from the keepers," the young woman said, surprising Gideon with a familiar Fordian accent. "I haven't seen you in, what, two weeks?" she continued as she set the plates down, pulled the whistling kettle from the stove and poured the steaming water into a waiting pot.

"Been busy," the dodger replied with a shrug. "You look—bigger."

"Yeah, part of the process. Millions of years of evolution, and this is the best we can do." She leaned on her side of the counter where the girl, after a brief hesitation, joined her, gesturing for Gideon to follow. The redhead gave Gideon a sharp look as he approached. "And who's your friend? A little tall for a dodger, isn't he?"

"I was shorter when I started," Gideon said and was rewarded by a sharper look than the first. So sharp, in fact, he felt a bit as if he were being dissected by her keen gray eyes.

"Another Ford native," she observed, studying him. "Far from home aren't you, soldier?"

"Likewise."

"This here's Jinna," the girl jerked her chin at the young woman. "Jinna, this is Gideon. He's okay, for a citizen."

"High praise from Mia," Jinna murmured.

"Your name is Mia?" he asked, glancing at the girl, who shrugged.

He then turned back to Jinna, who was also looking at Mia.

As he watched, Mia met Jinna's gaze, then Jinna's brows shot up, and Mia's hands rose, palms up, followed by a shrug.

Jinna sighed, then turned to Gideon. "You're welcome to take a seat anywhere," she said, then looked at Mia. "I've got some spare griddle cake batter and bacon that won't be missed."

"I can cover the cost of the meal," Gideon said, even as Mia's shoulders hunched, "though I do love a good griddle cake." He glanced at Mia who frowned, then shrugged.

"As long as you've loads of syrup," she muttered.

"A forest's worth," Jinna promised, shooting Gideon an appraising look. "Take a table, and I'll get your tea going."

Feeling very much dismissed, Gideon followed Mia to a booth, passing the aeronaut.

"Oy there, Mia," the airman greeted in the distinct brogue of the Campbell Isles.

"Oy back, Rory," Mia replied with a nod, telling Gideon that both were regulars.

And if Gideon were to judge from the glances the young man occasionally sent Jinna's way, he wasn't at Kit's for the food alone.

No doubt there was a story in those looks; a story that wouldn't be finished anytime soon, given that Rory was rising from the booth just as Jinna approached.

"No more tea?" she asked, hefting the pot she carried.

"Thanks, but no. Gotta get back to the *Errant*," he said as they passed each other by.

"Hold it right there, McCabe."

Rory stopped, turned to where Jinna stood by his table. "Is there a problem?"

"You left too much money." She picked up the stack of bills he'd tucked under his cup. "Again."

"I did nae such thing." Rory, to Gideon's amusement,

stuffed his hands in his pockets so he couldn't accept the cash Jinna was trying to foist back on him.

"It's twice what you owe." Jinna waved the bills at Rory.

"Consider it a down payment on my next meal."

"Rory . . ."

He shook his head and glanced at the clock on the wall. "Ach, will you look at the time! Best be off. Captain Pitte'll be pacing at the gangplank, he will."

"John hasn't paced a gangplank in, *ever*," Jinna countered.

Mia snorted, but Gideon felt a chill spread through his limbs on hearing the name of Rory's captain.

"*Oy*, what's wrong?" Mia hissed, reminding Gideon he wasn't alone here.

He shook his head.

"Aye, but it's been an odd day for the crew," Rory was explaining to Jinna. "Well, you saw."

"I did, but none of that excuses you leaving too much money," Jinna insisted, even as Rory retreated.

"How about this?" he countered. "How about you keep it safe for me until I've need of it?" Then, before Jinna could protest further, Rory spun around to make a dashing exit.

Or what would have been a dashing exit, if he hadn't misjudged and walked into the doorsill.

"That'll leave a mark," Mia muttered.

"I'm all right!" Rory called out before stumbling outside.

"Nutter," Jinna said with a fond sigh as she pocketed the cash and joined Mia and Gideon. "Sorry about that," she added. "Rory's an old—*oh!*" She stepped back as Gideon popped from the booth like a child's bounce ball. "What—" she began.

"What's his story?" Gideon asked, looming over her.

"Who? Rory?" Jinna glanced back at the door. "There isn't any—"

"Not Rory. The captain he mentioned. Pitte."

Gray eyes frosted over. "I don't see why it's any of your business."

"I fought with a Captain John Pitte at the Nasa Escarpment," he explained, which was true enough. "If it's the same guy, I'd like to catch up with him." Also true enough.

Jinna looked unconvinced, but after a moment relented with a short hiss. "Rory served under John on the *Kodiak*—until Nasa," she said, her own expression dark. "After the war, Rory, John, and another crewmate went into business together on an independent freighter and—" Jinna cut herself off this time, as Gideon was already moving to the front door.

He yanked it open and took a quick look outside, but the street was empty of any signs of the lovestruck Rory.

For a time, Gideon stood staring out at the night, then he glanced up to see Elvis peering down over the awning, his eyes gleaming as they reflected the warm light of the diner. "It's okay," Gideon said to the draco, then headed back inside. "I need a minute," he said to Mia, who was climbing out of the booth. Then, without another word, he strode quickly to the rear of the building, turning right at the hall where a sign pointed to the diner's restroom.

Once inside, he switched on the bathroom light, locked the door, and turned to the sink, where he leaned forward and gripped the edges of the basin as if grasping at a lifeline in a turbulent sea.

For a time he simply stood, barely noting the smooth, cool porcelain under his fingers. All he really knew was the ragged in and out of his breath, the echoes of plasma fire in a forest, and the old, old smell of smoke.

CHAPTER 9

Nasa Territory
Treicember 21, 1442 After Landing

THE SUNS WERE FINALLY SETTING WHEN A RESTLESS Gideon gave up on the idea of rest and headed for the edge of the escarpment.

"Who goes there?" Eitan's voice called softly.

"Quinn, Colonel of the twelfth," Gideon responded.

"Advance and be recognized. Have a care, sir," Eitan added as he stepped away from the tree he'd chosen for cover. "That last step is very final."

Gideon stepped closer, carefully, and peered over the side of the cliff.

It was, indeed, quite a drop.

It was also quite a sight, as the setting suns rendered the valley below into a sea of shadows, with only faint golden flickers from the river catching Tyche's last rays as she followed her sister, Nemesis, to sleep beneath the horizon.

"It is a beautiful place," Eitan observed as Gideon retreated to a safer viewing distance. "Temperate, fertile, plenty of room for wind farms, and water from the river." He indicated the Ares River, running quickly along the base of the cliff. "The keepers haven't prohibited the zone to human habitation," he added, "so how is it that none of the Coalition states have settled here?"

"No crystal?" Gideon guessed.

Eitan looked at him. "There is more to Fortune than crystal."

"Pretty sure there was more to Earth than oil," Gideon said, then paused, tilted his head. "Do you hear that?"

"Hear . . . ah," Eitan said as he too heard the telltale thrum of an approaching airship.

Gideon drew out his telescope and quickly found the 'ship, which was rapidly dropping on a west, southwest heading. He angled the scope upwards until he spied its colors, flying high on the crow's nest.

"She's one of ours," he said, then searched out the airship's designation. "The *Kodiak*." He handed the telescope to Eitan, then strode back toward the clearing. "Estelle," he called softly and was rewarded by the sight of a head popping up from a clump of abal shrubs. "Any incoming messages?"

"Not a ping, sir," she replied, tapping the headset she wore.

"She is a fine 'ship," Eitan observed, edging closer to the precipice to view the incoming vessel.

"Careful," Gideon echoed the lieutenant's earlier warning.

Eitan lowered the telescope and took a step back before raising the eyepiece again while asking, "Who commands her?"

Gideon searched his memory, found the name. "Captain Pitte," he said. "John Pitte."

"You've met?" Eitan asked.

"Not in person," Gideon said. "But the *Kodiak* provided air cover on one of our ops a few months before you joined us. Pitte was solid, maintained support under heavy ground-to-air fire.

Still," he added, staring at the incoming vessel, "I can't help but wonder what he's doing here with his very fine airship."

"Her cannon are moving into fire position," Eitan reported. "Should I call the company to arms?"

"We are not going to fire on one of our own vessels," Gideon said, though if one of their own vessels believed enemy forces were lurking in this grove, it'd be a bad day all around. "Radio, hail the *Kodiak* with my compliments. Let's say hello."

"Yes, sir," Estelle replied, sliding her headphones back in place.

At that point, Nbo jogged into the clearing, her own telescope in hand. "Any reason the *Kodiak*'s cannon are live?" she asked.

". . . hailing UCAS *Kodiak* under Captain Pitte, this is Corpsman Carver, 12th Company, 96th Infantry, please respond . . ." Estelle's voice drifted through the clearing.

"Technically, we are close to enemy territory," Eitan pointed out from his position, still studying the *Kodiak.*

"Technically, so are they," Gideon said. "Radio? Any response?"

"Nothing, sir," Estelle replied, holding the headset close. "Repeat, UCAS *Kodiak,* this is Corpsman Carver, Twelfth Company, do you read? Over." She flipped channels, tried again. "United Colonial Airship—"

"Smogging toxic Earth," Gideon muttered, joining Estelle. "Give me that," he gestured at the headset. "Hey, *Kodiak,*" he began as soon as he had the mic in place, "this is Colonel Gideon Quinn, 12th Company. Do you read? Over."

Static.

"Repeat, repeat, Captain Pitte . . ."

"They are taking aim," Eitan said.

"At what?" Nbo asked.

The lieutenant let the telescope drop to his side. "At us."

Gideon and Nbo were both ordering the company to find cover when the first shot struck the escarpment, just below where Eitan stood.

Then the lieutenant was falling and Gideon was rushing to grab him, but the shock wave from the blast knocked him on his ass.

Cursing, he scrambled to his feet to trail the rest of his fleeing soldiers, pausing only to grab Estelle's kit, keeping pace with her as she continued to hail the *Kodiak*.

All the while, all around them, plasma scored trees and earth.

Smoke stung Gideon's eyes and filled his lungs. His skin was blackened with soot, and the whine of cannon warred with the crack of exploding trees and the rustle and rumble of wildlife seeking safety.

Gideon spun Estelle away from a charging boar, then pulled the radio from her shoulder even as she coughed out another hail to the *Kodiak*. "Leave it."

"But, sir—"

"If Pitte was going to respond, he'd have done it by now," he yelled. "Run. That's an order, Corpsman!"

She looked as if she wanted to protest, but whatever she saw in Gideon's face had her swallowing, nodding, and turning to where Nbo was waving Walsie and Hamish through the conflagration.

As she darted away, Gideon turned and raised his rifle.

It was ridiculous, and he knew it, but he still took aim at one of the *Kodiak*'s cannon, hoping to at least cause the murdering airship some distress.

But before he could pull the trigger, the cannon fired, striking a nearby baobab tree, causing an explosion that knocked Gideon several meters before he landed hard.

Rolling onto his back, he lay blinking away ash and smoke

and saw the *Kodiak* soaring overhead, and the dancing pattern of its searchlights was the last thing Gideon saw before the dark rose to drag him under.

When he woke, some untold minutes later, every part of him hurt.

He took a breath to see if he could and tasted smoke, the tang of blood, and the ozone-heavy stench of crystal plasma.

Through the ringing in his ears, he heard the distant thrum of bees on the swarm, the distinctive creak of an airship's tie ropes, the harsh rasp of his own breath, and . . . a voice?

Yes, Gideon decided, someone was talking, but he couldn't understand what they were saying.

A little because of the aforementioned ringing ears, but mostly, he decided, because he was lying on his side facing Corpsman Estelle Carver, also on her side.

Her eyes were open wide, as if in surprise.

He figured she must have been at least a little shocked to find that big-ass piece of a baobab tree spitting from her chest.

The staring contest, such as it was, might have continued indefinitely, had not the sensation of someone pulling Gideon's rifle from under him pulled his gaze away from the very young, very dead, radio operator.

"What?" he asked, then coughed. "What?" he asked again, blinking up to find himself on the muzzle end of a rifle.

A rifle held by another young, but in this case very not dead, Air Corps provost tossing Gideon's weapon out of reach.

"What?" he said a third time before, out of sheer stubbornness, rolling to his knees and forcing himself to stand.

"Colonel Quinn, you will stand down," the voice of the prov pierced the remaining fog even as the youth hopped back, rifle to shoulder, Adam's apple bobbing with nerves.

"It's okay," Gideon managed, rocking back on his heels. "It's okay," he said again. "I'm standing down. See?" He held his hands out at his sides. "This is me, standing down."

The prov's trigger finger relaxed enough that Gideon took the chance to look around, hoping against hope that he'd already seen the worst, with Estelle.

He hadn't.

The grove was a mass of blackened stumps, through which a score of torch-bearing airmen moved, likely looking for survivors.

The only sign of his own company was Estelle, dead at his feet, and a pair of boots standing suspiciously empty about a dozen meters away.

"Where is Captain Pitte?" Gideon's voice was rough with more than smoke when he turned back to the provost. "Why did he fire on my company?"

"Given you were caught in the act of treason," a voice from the shadows replied, "I'd say you are in no position to be asking questions."

Gideon turned to his left to find General Jessup Rand stepping into the ruined clearing. "Treason?" he echoed.

"What else could explain your presence here?" Rand asked, coming to a halt beside the provost who became, if possible, more tense at the general's proximity. "You and your company in Nasa, en route to Coalition territory?"

"We are here on your orders," Gideon said, wishing the hammer currently pounding on the back of his skull would ease off already. "I mean, on General Satsuke's orders, after you seconded us to Spec Ops."

"I think I would remember something like that," Rand said. "Where are these orders?"

"Burned," Gideon admitted. "Also as ordered."

"Which is what I would say, if I were discovered committing treason."

"That," Gideon said, "is a complete load of draco sh—ow!" He swore and ducked as the provost, in a moment of panic, loosed a burst of plasma fire, singeing Gideon's shoulder before striking one of the last trees standing.

Gideon straightened and glared at the kid, who, to give him credit, looked apologetic. Gideon turned his attention back to Rand. "You have absolutely zero—"

"Proof?" This time it was Rand who interrupted, raising Gideon's field pack—from which he pulled a scarred document cylinder from the map pocket.

By now more airmen, provosts, and—thank the keepers—Corpsmen Freeman and Patel, were emerging from the smoke.

While the gathering crowd watched, Rand slid a rolled stack of papers from the cylinder. He gestured, and one of the airmen came forward with a torch as the general unrolled one of the pages.

"I'm no engineer," Rand said, holding one of the sheets up to the column of light, "but this looks a great deal like the specs for one of our plasma cannon. And this?" He pulled out a second sheet. "This is a map," he looked up, "marking the location of several key Colonial weapons depots. Ah, and here are plans for troop movements, mission specs . . . I'd imagine this is worth quite a lot to the Coalition brass."

"Sir?" Patel's voice was as hoarse as Gideon's and just as rife with disbelief.

Freeman just stood, staring, much as Gideon himself, while Rand rolled the papers back into the cylinder, then turned to Gideon. "It's a lucky thing the *Kodiak* intercepted you before you could meet your contact . . . Odile."

It was then, on hearing the code name Gideon had first read in Fort Molina, some months back, that Gideon felt the ground giving way beneath him, just as it had beneath Lieutenant Fehr. "No," he said.

"That can't be right," Freeman said, drawing Gideon's attention to find Hamish Costanza had joined Patel and Freeman, making three survivors, so far.

But where was Nbo? Gideon turned, looking for any sign of the sergeant, but all he saw were those empty boots and Estelle's unblinking gaze.

Which might be why, even as Rand ordered the young provost to take Gideon into custody, Gideon was already moving.

In the end, it took three aeronauts and the application of several shock sticks to get Gideon off the general, but not before Gideon left Rand with several cracked ribs, a bruised spleen, and a broken kneecap that would continue to ache every time the weather was damp.

His only regret, as the *Kodiak*'s crew hauled him off of the general, was he'd missed his shot at Captain Pitte.

CHAPTER 10

Mia winced as Gideon slammed the bathroom door.
"That's—"

"Where," Jinna said, "did you dig that one up?"

"He was supposed to be a mark," Mia admitted, meeting Jinna's frown with a shrug. "But things got twisty."

"*He* was a mark?" Disapproval gave way to amazement. "And how much of your fagin's booze had you drunk before you marked him?" she asked as she filled Mia's mug.

"It was the fagin's call," Mia replied. "And I know Gideon don't look like much—"

"I'll tell you what he looks like," Jinna cut in darkly. "He looks like trouble."

"He's a bit ragged, yeah, but—"

"I could give a comb for his looks. He's trouble because he's a convict."

Mia looked in the direction Gideon had gone. "How d'you know he's been in the nick?"

"Didn't you see the back of his hand? The right one?"

"His hand?" Mia squinted as she tried to picture either of Gideon's hands, but all she could recall was the map of scars over his torso, the scary shade of blue his lips had been before she and Elvis got him breathing again, and the way his eyes could sometimes seem hollow, as if only a part of a person were still living in that battered body. His hand, not so much. "What about it?"

"He's got a prison tattoo on the back of it." Jinna let out an exasperated huff. "I don't know how you could have missed the thing."

Well, first the man was drowning, and then he was attacked by some female with a gun, and then we were running, so maybe I missed a wee detail, Mia thought. "It's complicated," she said.

Jinna's eyebrows rose as she lowered herself into the booth opposite Mia. "How complicated?"

Mia glanced over Jinna's shoulder, but there was no sign of Gideon. "Right, then. It started when Ellison spied a man with a pet draco," she began and then laid out the story of her evening to date between sips of tea.

"He's lucky you were there," Jinna observed as Mia's tale concluded with their escape from the angry woman outside the Elysium Inn. "But even you should be able to see that soldier is trouble."

"And I'm such an upright citizen," Mia pointed out, tossing back the last of her tea.

"You could be, if you could get away from Ellison," Jinna observed as she refilled Mia's cup. "Has he been giving you trouble?"

"No more'n usual," Mia said, shoulders hunching.

"The usual is bad enough." To emphasize her point, Jinna nodded at the bruise on Mia's wrist. "It's not right, the way he treats his dodgers. You're almost of age. Old enough that if you were willing to forfeit your graduation shares, you could leave the hive and live with me. I could maybe get Sol to hire you here and—wait." She looked up at the sound of something scraping the diner's glass door. "What was that?"

Mia looked back at the diner's windows and saw it had started to rain again. "I bet it's Elvis," she said, sliding from the booth. "Must be getting lonely out there."

"Elvis?" With a little more effort, Jinna rose and, judging the teapot could use freshening, brought it along as she followed Mia to the front door. "Like the king from Earth?"

"Not exactly." Mia opened the door, letting in a rush of rainy wind and one exceptionally grumpy draco.

"Then wh—*eee!*" Jinna gave a delighted squeal, spinning to watch as Elvis flapped his way into the diner, coming to rest on the counter where he flapped the water from his wings and chittered angrily at Mia.

"Jinna, this is Elvis, Gideon's draco."

"Okay," Jinna said, still staring.

"He don't like rain," Mia added.

As if to prove it, Elvis gave a vigorous shake and then looked around, circling himself like a cat as his eyes skimmed the diner before coming back around to face Mia, to whom he gave a questioning chirp.

"If you're looking for Gideon, he's gone to the loo," Mia told him, pointing to the rear of the diner. "That way."

The draco apparently understood because, with a last flutter of rain from his wings, he jumped up, flapped in the direction she'd pointed, and swooped around the corner.

"Cor, that's a smart critter," Mia murmured.

"Maybe he needs the loo too," Jinna quipped, then sighed. "All right, take this." She handed Mia the teapot. "Let me lock the place up, and then I'll make you all some dinner."

Mia took the pot and started toward the counter pass-through while Jinna headed for the door, just as it slammed open again.

"I'm sorry, but we're closed," Jinna said coldly, and Mia turned to see her friend backing away from the three men and a woman who entered.

Mia knew two of the men and the woman, as they lived on the same fringes of society as her hive. Plus, anyone who'd seen Freya, Rolf, and Ulf Ohmdahl once would never forget the Stolichnayan triplets.

"I am sorry as well," said the fourth member of the party, a slender, silver-haired risto, whose deep brown skin and cold dark eyes contrasted vividly with the trio of blond mountains accompanying him. "Sorry to hear you've refused—again—my offer of a comfortable home for my grandchild."

"So sorry that you've brought help to convince me, Msr Del?" Jinna countered, shooting a cool glance at the towering Ohmdahls.

"That's *Minister* Del, and I believe we are past persuading," the risto said, flicking one elegant hand in Jinna's direction.

Ulf and Rolf took the cue, moving further into the diner while Freya remained at the door, her expression troubled.

Mia looked up as Rolf planted himself near her. "Rolf," she greeted her fellow miscreant. "How's your mum?"

"Mia." He nodded to the dodger. "Mama is being good." He glanced at his employer of the moment, then at Mia to add in a softer rumble, "But maybe you should be going now?"

"Yes, you should indeed be going," Del said, barely glancing at Mia. "This is a private matter."

"No, it isn't," Jinna countered. "Anything you have to say to me, you can say in front of witnesses, and then those witnesses," she jerked her chin up at Ulf, who'd settled into full looming posture at her side, "can mark me telling you, as I have told you nearly every swarming day for the past four months, you are *not* taking my child."

"Understandable, if misguided," Del replied. "Which is

why I've decided the best course of action is to bring you to my home, as a guest. I'm confident that by the time you come to term, you'll accept what's best for the child." He nodded to Ulf, who grumbled something in Stolichnayan.

But Mia knew Ulf hadn't reckoned with the likes of Jinna Pride because, even as he reached for her, she ducked under his arms and darted back to the main dining area, where she grabbed a mustard bottle.

"Move, you idiots," Del snapped.

They moved, Ulf following Jinna into the seating area and Rolf lumbering past Mia, clearly meaning to cut Jinna off at the far end of the diner.

Which was when Mia remembered the teapot in her hands.

Or, it was in her hands until she threw it at Rolf.

"Sorry!" She winced as the pot bounced off Rolf's shoulder before shattering on the floor. "*Really* sorry," she added as Rolf turned in her direction while, in the middle of the room, Jinna shot a squirt of mustard into Ulf's eye.

"That was not nice," Rolf said over his brother's pained gurgle.

At the door, Freya took a step forward, then stopped and let out a gasp of surprise as, out of nowhere, Elvis descended on Rolf in a flurry of wings and talons.

A splintering crack had Mia darting away from Elvis and Rolf to see Gideon holding the leg of a chair, and Ulf thudding to the floor like a poleaxed aurochs.

"Oy, Gideon!" Mia crowed, drawing Gideon's attention.

"Hey," he waved the chair leg in her direction, then looked at Jinna. "How are you?"

"Angry," she said.

Gideon could relate, given the mood he'd been in when Elvis had come scratching at the bathroom door.

Now he looked at the small, fierce woman at his side and jerked his chin at the guy Elvis was harassing. "Do you want to do the honors, or shall I?"

"Carry on, soldier." Jinna waved him on, but kept the mustard to hand as Gideon clambered over the man he'd knocked senseless.

Mia, he was pleased to see, had already retreated to relative safety on the other side of the counter.

A click of the tongue sent Elvis leaping to perch near Mia, so there was no one in the way when Gideon came flying at his target, chair leg slamming across the man's back.

"Ulf's up!" Mia called from her position.

"Copy that," Gideon replied as he ducked under a blindly swinging fist before thrusting the makeshift club into his opponent's gut. As the man crumpled forward, he delivered a quick elbow strike to the his temple, then spun, chair leg swinging to crack open the approaching Ulf's cheek.

"Mind your seven!" Jinna warned at the same time Elvis hissed.

Gideon, still in motion, reversed his swing to thwack the incoming woman's arm, then bounced back to smack Ulf behind the ear, dropping him again before spinning to his sister, the last triplet standing.

"Quit the field," he said, brandishing the chair leg before adding a softer, "*Please.*"

Rubbing her arm, Freya looked at her fallen brothers, then at Jinna and finally at Gideon. "As you say." Then she turned away to minister to the wounded.

"Cor, Gideon! That was completely badass," Mia called from the other side of the counter. "I could'a sold tickets."

Gideon flashed her a grin, then turned to where the poncy

risto stood, staring. His fingers tightened on the chair leg, and he took a step forward.

"I wouldn't, if I were you," the risto said. "Unlike these lunks you've put down, I have friends. Powerful friends."

Gideon didn't move but held the risto's gaze—long enough to see the first skitterings of fear in those dark eyes. Only then did he look at Jinna, who was still in the middle of the dining room, clutching the mustard dispenser like a shooter.

"He's probably right," she admitted, her voice tight.

Gideon turned to the risto. "Guess it's your lucky day."

The risto managed a viper-like smile before dipping his head in Jinna's direction. "We will speak again," he told her. "And if I may? Try to get more rest. It wouldn't do for the mother of my heir to take ill." Then he spun on one heel and took himself out of the diner.

"I should be feeling bad about this job going swarm," the blond woman said as Ulf groaned at her side, "but I really do not like that man."

"You and me both, sister," Gideon said.

Behind them, Jinna kicked a fallen plate.

CHAPTER II

While Mia and Jinna triaged the Ohmdahls and Gideon gathered up bits of broken table, Freya explained how the triplets came to be working for Killian Dell.

"His man of business found us in a local pub," she said, holding a cloth to Rolf's temple. "This man said the mother of Del's grandchild was sickly, but too proud to accept his generosity. He made it sound like we were doing a service for a woman in need."

"We should have known better," Rolf determined, wincing. "What risto is going to be hiring us?"

"Politicians." Ulf spat the word, then focused on Jinna, at his side. "I hope you can forgive us."

"Give me a day," Jinna said, managing a smile, but Gideon didn't think the shine in her eyes came from the sharp odor of the antiseptic she was applying to Ulf's cuts.

Soon enough, the triplets were cleaned up and, with a few of Gideon's starbucks, limped off to rethink their life choices at their favorite pub.

Once he'd locked the door after the departing Ohmdahls,

Gideon turned to see Jinna had begun sweeping up broken crockery. "Tell me about Killian Del."

"It's complicated," Jinna said, blowing a strand of hair from her face.

He looked at Mia, who had found some leftover bacon in the kitchen and was now sharing it with Elvis, which was nice for Elvis but also reminded Gideon how hungry he was.

"Jinna had a thing with Liam Del—Killian Del's son," Mia explained as Gideon joined her at the counter. "And then *their* thing turned into *that* thing." She nodded at the bulge under Jinna's apron. "And Del thinks 'cause his son's bits are involved, he should get the baby."

Gideon looked at Jinna.

"Okay, so maybe not that complicated," she admitted.

"Complicated or not, I don't think it's safe for you to stay here," Gideon observed, grabbing a piece of bacon from Mia's plate.

"I don't have anywhere else to go," Jinna said, focusing intently on the broken bits of plate she was brushing into a pile.

Gideon swallowed the bit of bacon he'd snagged. "No family back in Ford?"

"Lost in the 'forty-seven push." She shrugged. "I'd already joined up, so I was in Epsilon, in basic training, when Macintosh fell."

"What division?" he asked as she resumed her sweeping.

"Seventy-Second Airborne."

"Recon?"

"Demolitions."

"Cool," Gideon said, swallowing the last of his bacon. "So how'd you end up in a diner in Nike City?"

She visibly tensed, and Gideon waited for her to tell him to mind his own hive, but then she gave a short shrug and kept sweeping as she explained, "Peace happened. And soon after the accords were signed, our 'ship—Liam, Rory, and I all served on the *York*—moored in Nike for liberty. One night, after Rory left the Rigging, Liam and I—we—well." She glanced up at Mia. "One thing led to another, and then another." She nodded at her swollen belly. "I decided I'd done my bit for home and colony, put in my papers, and got myself a job."

"But the father—Liam—died," Gideon guessed, and she nodded. "How?"

"The *York* flew a research team into the Amazons and never came back." She pushed the last of the broken dishes into a pile. "The brass figured the 'ship ran into a storm, or a mountain. Either way, no one on the *York* got to enjoy the peace for very long.

"He was a good man," she added, not looking at Gideon. "And so excited about the baby. Excited enough that he must have told his father, because only one day after I learned Liam was gone, Killian Del was at my door, demanding *his* heir."

"And he's not the type to take no for an answer," Gideon surmised.

"I don't believe the word exists in his vocabulary."

"I'm familiar with the type," Gideon said. "What about the law? Have you tried swearing out a complaint?"

At this, both Mia and Jinna laughed, but not the ha-ha, funny kind of laugh.

Gideon looked from one to the other. "I can see I'm missing something."

"You're not from Nike," Mia said.

"So?"

"So you probably don't have much idea how things work here," Jinna told him, reaching for the dustpan she'd set on a nearby table.

"No, I don't." Gideon stepped forward, took the dustpan

from her, and knelt to hold it in front of the pile of broken bits. "Why don't you enlighten me?"

She managed a small smile, then began to sweep the mess into the pan he held. "It's not the cops' fault," she began over the clatter of dishes. "Most of them are like us—working people who want to keep peace in the city. The problem is district ministers with different ideas of whose peace is being kept."

"The ministers are on the take?" Gideon guessed, looking up at Jinna.

"Some of them," Jinna said.

Mia, now spinning back and forth on her stool, snorted.

"More than some," Jinna amended, stepping back from the filled dustpan. "And Killian Del isn't just a district minister. He also sits on a number of committees, including law enforcement and budgeting, which means—"

"He's got the police force, or at least the police force's cash, in his pocket," Gideon concluded, rising with the filled dustpan in his hand. He looked back at Jinna. "You can't stay here."

Jinna looked over the damage, and as he watched, the anger that had been sustaining her seemed to drain, leaving in its wake a sort of exhausted sadness. "I doubt I'll be allowed to stay after this." She looked at Mia. "Guess we won't have the chance to be flatmates after all."

"Ellison wouldn't have let it happen, anyway," Mia said, looking almost as deflated as Jinna.

"Let's handle one problem at a time," Gideon said. "The first issue is getting you somewhere Del can't find you."

"You did hear what we said about Del's influence?" she asked, taking the dustpan away and heading behind the counter.

Frustrated, Gideon shoved his hands in his pockets, and let his thoughts go to town.

Most of the thoughts—the sort that said this affair was none of his business—he let float along past.

A few, regarding potential exit strategies for the young mother, he discarded as being too risky, too expensive, and—given the long arms of Killian Del—too likely to fail.

What she needs, one thought said, clearing its throat enough to set the other thoughts to a dull mumble, *is a friend in high places.*

No shit, he thought back. *Got a contact in the city parliament?*

Not politically *higher*, the thought prodded. Literally *higher*. Then, as it seemed Gideon was unable to keep up with himself, added, *Remember Rory?*

Rory the gawky aeronaut? Rory, who's half in love with the girl? Rory, who works on an independent—

"Freighter!" he said aloud and was rewarded by two pairs of eyes—three, counting Elvis's—looking at him like he was talking to himself.

Which—no, no reason to let them know that.

"Rory might be able to help," he said to Jinna. "We need to talk to him."

Which also meant talking to Rory's captain.

And at that thought, all the other thoughts fell silent.

CHAPTER 12

As Gideon began to lay out his plan to Jinna, Killian Del entered a townhouse on Chaucer Street where he'd been invited to dine with the owners and a select number of their acquaintance.

Killian had sent his regrets for dinner, expecting to be occupied with settling Jinna Pride into his own home, but given how the evening had turned out, he'd decided to stop by and join in the postprandial conversation.

As he stepped inside the foyer, the odors of rain were replaced by leather, wood, beeswax, and the echo of a woman's spicy perfume.

Rich scents; scents Killian associated with power.

"Thought for certain you'd stood us up, Kill."

Speaking of power . . . Killian turned to see a man of average height, average weight, and average golden-brown skin arriving to greet him.

In fact, nothing about Jessup Rand spoke of power, but between his rank, his wealth, and his family connections, the general could likely do more damage with a word than most could with a crysto-plas repeater.

"My plans misfired," Killian explained. "It caused some delays."

"As long as you made it," Jessup said, leading the way into the parlor, where several of Nike's movers and shakers were comfortably ensconced amongst the deep-cushioned chairs and the buttery leather sofa.

Jessup's wife, Celia, stood in front of the grand fireplace, gesturing with the glass in her hand. Her dark hair was cut at a cheekbone-enhancing angle, which was echoed by the slash of her red, one-shouldered gown.

She was posed, as if on the stage, as she regaled her seated guests with yet another of her shocking stories.

Celia Rand, Killian had often thought, collected scandals as avidly as she collected the artifacts scattered whimsically throughout the room.

"She is a vision, is she not?" Jessup asked, but the question was soft, as if he were addressing himself. "Come along, then," he added as if shaking off the vision that was his wife. "I'll set you up."

Killian followed Jessup to the sideboard where an ancient bottle and two empty cans, all displaying the faintest traces of their Earth manufacture, were displayed amongst the prosaic cut-glass decanters.

Jessup selected one of the decanters and poured two glasses before handing one to Killian, who raised a brow at the three fingers of single malt in the heavy tumbler.

"You'll need to catch up with the rest of us," Jessup explained.

"And who are you catching up with?" Killian asked, as Jessup had been just as generous with his own liquor.

"A dutiful host doesn't allow his guests to drink alone." Jessup raised the glass in a toast.

"A point," Killian said as he touched glasses with his host—

and promptly downed half of the liquor.

"Keepers, man!" Jessup gaped. "I didn't mean catch up on the instant!"

"My apologies," Killian said, somewhat roughly, as the whiskey burned its way through his system. "The evening has been something of a trial."

"Yes, well, that sort of thing does seem to be going around," Jessup murmured.

Killian, despite the earlier disappointment, was willing to be diverted by his friend's statement. "Trouble with the peace accords?" he asked, grasping at the most likely candidate for Jessup's unease.

"If only." Jessup topped off both drinks. "Though it's true that the negotiations are dragging. Nine months after the treaty's signed, and we're still dancing around the crystal issue."

"I'd also heard there was some contention over the Adian slave trade," Killian remarked.

"That too," Rand agreed.

"But if, as you say, the talks aren't the problem?" Killian prompted.

Before answering, Jessup glanced at his wife, who'd reached the climax of her tale and was now basking in a round of laughter and applause.

Seeming satisfied, he stepped closer to Killian and turned slightly away from the crowd in the center of the room. "I recently learned that a difficulty I'd thought permanently resolved has resurfaced," he said quietly. "In fact, it resurfaced in Nike earlier this evening."

"A difficulty?"

"A man," Jessup clarified.

"Anyone I'm familiar with?" Killian asked over a sip.

"Only if you were paying attention to news from the ranks six—no, closer to seven years ago, now. News of an infantry colonel being court-martialed for treason and attempted murder of a superior officer."

Killian's brows rose. "I take it you were the superior officer in question?"

"My knee still aches on damp mornings," Jessup confirmed. "And in Nike, every morning is damp." He raised his glass and took a gulp as hefty as the one for which he'd berated Killian earlier. "But the officer confessed to the—to his crime—and was sentenced to Morton because of it."

Even brimful of whiskey, Killian couldn't miss Jessup's quick correction. "And you believe he's here, in Nike?"

"I *know* he is," Jessup said, his expression grim. "My contact in the prison telephed the news on the day Gideon Quinn was released."

"And you believe this man means to—wait." Killian raised his glass, one finger extending to point at Jessup. "You say his name is *Gideon* Quinn?"

"A name I've cursed daily for seven years," Jessup said, then his eyes tracked over Killian's shoulder, his expression changing so drastically Killian knew someone was approaching. "Darling," Jessup greeted his wife, "Killian's just been telling me about his difficult evening."

Killian took the hint. For whatever reason, Jessup didn't want his wife to know of this problematic colonel. "As you may know," he took his cue, turning to Celia, "the mother of my grandchild is proving difficult. After months of arguments and tantrums, I'd finally made arrangements on my own to establish her in my own home until the birth of the child."

Celia made appropriate noises as she poured more whiskey for the men, listening with gratifying interest as Killian vented the story of the evening's escapade.

And when he came to the point of the tall blue-eyed soldier appearing out of nowhere to best the Ohmdahls, he turned his gaze to Jessup. "I confess myself shocked to find a man of the infantry—and a colonel at that—involved with a woman of such character."

Jessup's facial expression remained calm, but Killian saw his eyes sharpen.

"Yes, yes, quite shocking." Celia seemed to wave the seedier implications aside. "I am more impressed by the way you described his eyes," she recalled with a delighted shiver. "How vividly you tell the story, Kill."

"Perhaps I was inspired by my hostess," Killian said with the smallest of bows.

"Celia," Jessup broke into the moment, "it looks as if the Porters are leaving. Would you do the courtesies?"

There was the slightest of pauses, no more than three beats of the heart, as she met her husband's gaze.

"Of course," she said, then turned to Killian. "Kill, thank you for confiding in us. If there is anything we can do to help you with the matter, I hope you'll not hesitate to ask."

Killian, watching her walk away, couldn't help but think that Jessup was a lucky man.

He turned to his host, meaning to say just that, but Jessup was also watching his wife, his expression so raw, so conflicted, it was all Killian could do to keep his own features bland as yesterday's eggs when Jessup's focus finally returned to him. "Vivid as my story was, I left out one vital element." He paused, looked at Celia, then back at Jessup. "I did not tell you the soldier's name."

Jessup waited, saying nothing.

"The urchin called him Gideon."

CHAPTER 13

"Where did you get the car?"

At Jinna's question, Gideon patted the hood of the Edsel Comet he'd found while she and Mia had gone to Jinna's flat to pack up a few belongings. "Borrowed it," he said, taking Jinna's carryall and tossing it into the back seat.

Jinna's glare moved to Gideon. "Does the owner know you borrowed it?"

"Nope," he admitted. "And if we can get it back soon enough, he never will. Shall we?" he asked, opening the passenger door with a flourish.

"Best get on," Mia said, sliding into the back seat.

"This is insane," Jinna huffed, but she did get in the car, then let out a soft laugh as Elvis hopped in after.

Even with the sprightly Edsel, the airfield's main gates were locked by the time they arrived. Luck remained on their side, however, as a pair of tipsy aeronauts toppled out of the late-night tram and Gideon's party followed them through the personnel gate.

"All I'm saying," the first aeronaut declared, "is life on

airships'd be a deal simpler if we had us some matter transporters like they had back inna day."

"You're sauced." His friend tried to slap the speaker's arm and hit the air instead, proving the sauce had not been selective in its targets. "Ain't so nuch thing as matter tranposters. Never 'ave been."

Gideon—with Elvis on his shoulder and Jinna's carryall in his hand—shared a wide-eyed glance with Mia.

"A'course there were," drunk number one insisted. "S'in all'a records, ain't it?"

"Them's ficshun," drunk number two opined. "If all'a books our aassestors brought wiff'em was a record, we'd be arse to elbows in fairies, an kaiju, an' coffee."

"Oh my," Gideon whispered.

Jinna elbowed him.

"I don' know how you can close your mind so, Ken." Drunk number one shook his head—and almost face planted because of it.

"An' I don' know how you can hear past the wind whislin' through that empty skull, John."

At this point, the pair turned off toward the passenger liners, and though Gideon feared they were going to come to blows (or, given the level of sobriety, near misses), at least they'd be doing it far, far from him.

"I never did believe in coffee," Mia said as they wove their way through the anchored cargo vessels.

"I've always wanted to," Gideon said.

"There it is." Jinna pointed, and all three froze, staring at the uniqueness that was the *Errant*.

"It flies?" Mia looked from the ship to Jinna and back again.

Gideon shook his head. "If it does, I bet they serve coffee, too."

"She's nae much to look at, but she's a rare lass," the inimitable Rory called as he scrambled down from the engine on which he'd been crouched, a torch in one hand and a spanner in the other.

"I can believe that," Gideon murmured.

"Maybe this was a bad idea," Mia said.

"What's a bad idea?" Rory asked, coming to a landing near Jinna. "And for that matter, what are you lot doing out and about so late?"

"It's—" Jinna began.

"Jinna's in trouble," Mia said at the same time.

"Trouble?" Rory spun to face Jinna. "What sort of trouble? Wait, you're dead pale," he added. "You'll come inside and have a cuppa while you tell us what's what." Already, he was leading the small party around to the rear gangplank.

"Rory," a male voice emerged from the gondola as they approached, "have you made any progress on that engine pod?"

"I've got the connection rewired," Rory told the newcomer, still shepherding Jinna toward the gangplank, "but there's another problem."

"I'm not sure we can afford any more problems on this job," the man said as he stepped onto the tarmac. "Oh. Pardon me, Jinna. I didn't realize Rory had company." His gaze shifted to Mia, then Gideon and Elvis, before returning his attention to the mechanic. "What kind of problem are we talking about?"

"Jinna's got some sort of trouble," Rory explained, then looked back at the others. "This is John Pitte, captain of the *Errant*. John, this is Jinna's friend, Mia, and . . ."

"Pleased to make your acquaintance." John's easy smile warmed further at the girl's answering grin.

"Sorry," Rory apologized as he looked at the soldier. "I didn't catch your name."

"I didn't throw it," Gideon replied, his eyes locked on Pitte, who, meeting his gaze, moved closer, leaving Gideon to wonder how the man who'd murdered his company could look so—benign? "Gideon Quinn," he said, "Commander of the—"

"Twelfth Company," Pitte cut in, and Gideon thought he saw the man shudder.

"John?" Rory's question bounced off the tension wire connecting the two men.

Pitte blinked, then looked down, then met Gideon's gaze. "You kept the coat?"

"You didn't," Gideon noted.

"No," John said. "It didn't feel . . . right."

Which was all John Pitte had time to say, because that was when Gideon's already thin hold on control snapped and, with a rushing shove that sent Elvis flying, slammed Pitte back, head-first into the *Errant*'s hull, where he then grabbed the stunned captain by the throat with both hands and began to squeeze.

Behind his eyelids, he read the names etched on the wall of his cell. . . *Eitan Fehr*. . . *Estelle Carver* . . . *Bertie Walsingham* . . . *Nbo Mulowa*—

"Six of my company died on his order," he growled at the cries of protest.

"N-Not mine," Pitte's voice creaked out as an arm, presumably Rory's, snaked around Gideon's own throat in an attempt to pull him back.

But Gideon wasn't letting go. Six dead soldiers lent him more than enough strength to hold on. "Liar."

"No," Pitte managed to force out. "My fault, but not... mine."

"I don't believe you."

"You should." A voice Gideon remembered—a voice he'd

last heard on the Nike Escarpment—spoke. *Listen,* the voice continued, but lost to reason, Gideon shook off the ghost in his head.

"Let him go," another voice snapped from behind, this one unknown, female, and supremely angry.

He might have ignored the order, but it was accompanied by the press of something cold, metallic, and humming at the base of his skull.

"Let him go," she said again, "or I will be decorating the hull with your brains."

"Jag—" Pitte gasped.

"Gideon," Mia's voice, strangely thick, followed.

"I won't bother to count to three," the woman said.

From somewhere nearby, Elvis let out a low croon.

All of which had weight, no doubt; but it was Pitte's expression—one that had no name, but which Gideon had seen in countless mirrors since that day at Nasa—that tipped the scales and, with a shuddering breath, Gideon loosened his grip and stepped away.

Then, as if from a great distance, he watched Pitte slump down onto a supporting shoulder—a shoulder that belonged to a man Gideon had seen fall at the Nasa Escarpment. Staring, his hand half rose, then fell again.

He heard the sound of someone crying and realized it was Mia.

He began to turn, to tell her . . . something . . . when he felt a sharp thunk at the back of his head, and then he too was slumping, with no shoulder to stop him, all the way to the cold wet of the tarmac.

"Jagati, that was hardly necessary," Gideon heard Pitte's voice rasp.

"Were you without oxygen long enough to suffer brain

damage?" the woman—presumably Jagati—snapped. "Because that was absolutely necessary."

"She's not wrong," Dani said, leaning over him on the wet tarmac, before adding, "You have such a way with people."

Her dark hair was loose this time, spilling down in a curtain, closing him off from everyone else.

"It's a skill," Gideon told her. He reached out to touch that hair, the midnight rain of it, and saw his hand was still shaking from the effort of nearly murdering a man.

"No," she said, easing away from his touch.

"What?" he asked as her gaze cooled. "What's wrong?"

"You," she told him. "This." She waved a hand in Pitte's direction. "What you're becoming. What Jessup Rand is turning you into."

"Rand's not turning me into anything," he said, then watched her tilt her head in that particular way she had, and cursed. "Fine, what's he turning me into, then?"

"Him," she said simply.

"Which would be bad," Gideon said, amazed at the coldness in his own voice, "if being Rand weren't working out so well for him."

At that, her eyes dropped, and she faded into the rain, leaving Gideon with nothing but the echoes of his hate.

CHAPTER 14

"Hallo!"

The greeting, as brittle as it was chipper, had Gideon groaning as it shredded through the fog of his concussed dream.

"Still feeling poorly, are we?"

Gideon cracked an eye open to see Rory, crouched at his right side. "Poorly is how a guy feels when he's hung over," he said. "What I'm feeling is an order of magnitude past that."

"Good!" Rory said, giving Gideon a vigorous slap on the shoulder before setting a cold pack, somewhat less vigorously, against the back of his head until Gideon's right hand rose to hold it in place. "That means you'll think twice before trying a cocked-up move like that again."

Gideon wasn't so sure of that, but at the moment he had other concerns, first among them not being able to recall precisely what those concerns were.

Then another man crouched down on the wet tarmac to Gideon's left, and he remembered one of them. "I saw you die."

"You saw me fall," Eitan Fehr corrected, his dark hair falling forward, a wavier echo of Dani's. "A bad fall, but into the river, so not fatal."

Gideon held the other man's gaze, then looked down to where Eitan's left hand used to be. He looked up again.

"That happened later, in Adia."

"Adia," Gideon echoed, then muttered a curse because the state of Adia had resurrected some of Ancient Earth's less savory practices when it came to dealing with prisoners of war. "I'm sorry."

Eitan looked down at the hand that wasn't there. "You could not have known." He paused. "I learned others of our company were not so fortunate. Mulowa, Walsingham, Carver, Duvagne . . . Siska."

The hesitation reminded Gideon that Cadet Siska and Lieutenant Fehr had shared a tent from time to time. "Their trees were planted in the Epsilon forest," he said. "Along with Hamish. He fell at Asgard, a couple years back, covering his company's retreat."

Eitan's expression tightened, then he let out a soft huff. "He was a good cook."

"And a terrible singer," Gideon recalled, forcing himself to a sitting position and immediately regretting it.

Eitan laid a steadying hand on his shoulder, then both men looked at Rory, who cleared his throat. "I'll just get back to yon engine pod, shall I?" The young man sprang to his feet.

"Wait," Gideon said, as moving had jostled a few other concerns to the front of his brain. "Where's Mia, and Elvis? And Jinna?"

"The lasses are aboard, having a cuppa," Rory said. "And who's Elvis?"

A croon and a flapping of wings on high had all three men looking up to the top of the gondola, where Elvis had perched. His eyes, fixed on Gideon, gleamed in the *Errant's* running lights. "That's Elvis," Gideon said. "It's okay," he added to the restless draco. "I mean, I was an idiot, but it's okay now." He paused, looked at Rory. "It is okay, isn't it?"

Rory turned from his contemplation of the draco to meet Gideon's questioning gaze. "I suppose that'll be up to John to decide. Be sure to keep that cold pack in place," he added before walking away.

Eitan waited for Rory to move out of earshot before speaking again. "You have questions," he said to Gideon.

"A few," Gideon replied, wincing as he pressed the ice to the knot on his head.

Eitan nodded, looked away, then back. "I won't speak of Adia."

"Understood," Gideon replied. "So let's move on to how it is you're now working for the man who shot you off a cliff?"

"John did not fire those cannons."

"Fired, ordered fired." Gideon waved that off. "It's all the same thing."

"Except Captain Pitte was not the one giving those orders," Eitan explained. "The orders came from General Rand. John refused to comply, so Rand had him forcibly removed from command, court-martialed, and dishonorably discharged."

"Is that what Pitte told you?" Gideon asked.

"No," the voice Gideon had last heard ordering him to release Pitte broke in. "That's what I told him."

Gideon looked up to see the woman who'd arrived, crate propped against one hip and a shooter holstered on the other.

"She explained it all, just in time to prevent me killing John," Eitan confirmed.

"And you believed her?"

"I did, once John allowed me to sense the truth."

Gideon chewed on that for a second, then looked up at the glaring Jagati. "Thanks for stopping me," he said, at the same time wondering how many times she'd been forced to step between her captain and vengeance-minded soldiers.

Her eyes narrowed, then she gave an ill-humored shrug and turned her attention to Eitan. "I got some dirt on the grand-daddy, Killian Del, from Alvaro at the mail office."

"Alvaro knows everyone," Eitan murmured.

"And their second cousin," she affirmed. "But between what he says about Del and the smog-fest our job has turned into, we need to get aloft, ASAP."

"Understood."

She gave Gideon one last fulminating glare, then stomped up the gangplank and into the 'ship.

"She's impressive," Gideon said, after a beat. Certainly, she'd made an impression on him.

"She is at that," Eitan agreed. "Jagati is also a good friend."

"I'll have to take your word for it, seeing how she pretty much hates me." Then he looked more closely at Eitan, still in that animal-like crouch. "I bet you have some questions of your own."

Eitan nodded. "When I returned to the Colonies, I not only learned who of our company died," he said. "I learned you were in prison, for treason. That you confessed." His eyes were too dark to read as he looked at Gideon.

"You heard right. I did confess to treason."

Eitan's breath sucked in, then hissed out. "Why?"

"It's kind of a long story," Gideon said.

Eitan studied Gideon a moment, then he looked up, and Gideon followed his gaze to where Elvis was still watching. "Will you, or your friend, object to a sensing? It would go much faster and likely be less confusing."

Gideon's breath caught, and he just prevented a wince because his last experience with a sensitive hadn't ended well. Not through any fault of hers, or his, for that matter, but still . . .

But this was Eitan, the first of Gideon's company to fall, and a man who, by all appearances, had had a worse time of it than Gideon. "Go for it," he said.

Eitan gave a short nod, then laid his hand against the side of Gideon's head. "Remember," he murmured softly.

Gideon wanted to say he'd never forgotten, but even as the word echoed through his thoughts, he felt the sear of plasma burns, the ache of concussion.

The next breath he took smelled of allusteel and sweat, and when his hand clutched at his side, he felt the rough nap of a blanket.

Gideon's eyes opened to a dull gray ceiling, and he knew he was once again in the brig of the UCAS *Kodiak*, the day after half his company had died.

Nbo, he thought, his throat closing with rage. Eitan, Estelle . . .

Breathe, he heard/felt Eitan's voice. *This is only a memory.*

Memory, Gideon echoed the gentle remonstrance. *Right.*

You are not alone this time, Eitan reminded him, and bolstered by the other man's unseen presence, Gideon rose from his bunk on hearing a door creak open, allowing a limping General Rand into the brig.

Gideon continued to follow the path of his memory by walking over to the bars of his cell, where he waited for Rand to come to a stop in front of him.

The general was leaning on a cane, and his leg had been immobilized in a brace.

Probably made getting up and down ladder a bitch, Gideon thought. "Nice cane," he said.

Gideon couldn't be certain, but it felt as if Eitan found that funny.

Rand did not. "You are going to plead guilty to treason, desertion, and assaulting a superior officer."

Gideon stared. "I really don't see that happening." He considered. "Well, except for that last."

"I rather think you will," Rand told him. "Particularly given the overwhelming evidence against you."

"The manufactured evidence," Gideon countered. "You planted that intel in my pack."

"Why would I do that?" Rand asked. "By the way, we've contacted Special Operations, and General Satsuke assures me her division issued no orders to your company. Your supposed witnesses are either dead or accused with you, and you already have a history of ignoring orders, breaking regulations . . . murdering enemy officers." A thin smile accompanied that last. "Beyond all that, the civilian airship you claim transported you to Nasa has yet to answer any of our hails."

Gideon's jaw, already clenched to the point of pain, twitched. "Dead or paid off?"

"That is a question," Rand said, then changed the subject. "Then, of course, there is all this." He held up the cane, gestured to the livid bruise on the right side of his face. "You'd be amazed how much weight aggravated assault can add to a case of treason. So much weight," he added, "I am within my mandate to order a battlefield execution. Not for you. Your rank guarantees you the right to trial, but I can, and will, have every surviving member of the Twelfth Company shot at dawn."

Gideon felt Eitan's rage twining with his own and had to grip the bars to steady himself.

"A terrible fate for those six soldiers," Rand continued, as he had at the time. "Especially if they were only following their traitorous colonel's orders. And," he added, stepping closer to the bars, "in case the lives of your enlisteds aren't sufficient motivation, I'm given to understand you have a certain fondness for one Lieutenant Indani Solis stationed on the *Phalanx*."

"Wait," Gideon said.

"So easy for a jump to go wrong in the middle of a firefight," Rand continued. "Lines fail, weapons misfire . . . accidents happen." He paused, studying Gideon. "I see I have your attention."

"*Yes*." The word squeezed through a jaw so tight it ached.

"And you understand just how many lives are at stake here."

"Are they alive? Is Dani—are they all still alive?"

"You doubt me?"

"What do you think?" Gideon's hands slammed against the bars, and there was a cold satisfaction in seeing Rand flinch. "Are. They. Alive?"

"For now." Rand's response came out more as a hiss than as words. "But unless you take responsibility for the crimes of which you have been accused, what remains of your company will be witnessing their last sunrise in the next two hours, and soon after, Lieutenant Solis will be making her final jump."

Gideon's heart sped. His breath hitched.

Easy, Eitan reminded him.

"And what happens when I'm in prison and Odile keeps selling our secrets to the enemy?" Gideon asked; not that he expected an answer, but it appeared Jessup Rand was full of surprises.

"If this Odile is even half competent, they'll have changed their code name the second you discovered it at Fort Molina. Besides, given how many spies are operating on both sides of the conflict, one more or less won't signify."

Gideon stepped closer to the bars. "It will if it turns out you're the real Odile, using my confession for cover."

"You dare suggest I'd betray the colonies? The Corps?" Rand asked, with legitimate affront.

Which was beyond enough. "You didn't have any problem betraying my company," Gideon began, but then stepped back as Rand's expression shifted, changing in a blink from triumph to a self-loathing so ravenous it had the spit drying in Gideon's mouth.

"Do you have the least idea," Rand asked as Gideon stared, shocked, "the *least* idea what I've done because of you?"

"I know exactly what you've done," Gideon replied. "What I don't know is why."

"Don't you?" Rand asked as the loathing of self gave way to a livid, living hatred of the man imprisoned before him, then he reached into his pocket and withdrew a thin piece of fabric in vivid red which, unfurling, released a subtle, spicy scent. "You should never have touched her," he said before crumpling the silk in one hand and turning to make his halting way out of the brig, leaving Gideon alone with the lingering odor of Celia Rand's perfume and the memory of her body pressed close against his.

The door to the brig clanged shut, closing on the memory as Gideon's eyes opened, then closed again.

Eitan dropped his hand from Gideon's head to rest on his shoulder.

"I'm good," Gideon lied to the backs of his eyelids.

"As you say," Eitan murmured, but he released his grip on Gideon.

Gideon sighed and opened his eyes.

"Did anyone actually believe you were Odile?" Eitan asked.

"Some," Gideon said, then added without thinking, "Dani never believed it."

"Lieutenant Solis is wise," Eitan murmured.

"But the brass accepted my confession of treason," Gideon continued. "Why wouldn't they? Rand was right about one thing; my jacket was stuffed with evidence of me disobeying orders, going rogue, murdering enemy officers—"

"That wasn't murder," Eitan cut in. "It was retribution."

"Tenjin didn't think so," Gideon said, recalling the officer who had led the inquiry of a mission gone swarm. "But it didn't help my case that I'd been tortured in that Ducati cell."

"The court believed you'd been turned, at Ducati," Eitan surmised.

"And I let them believe it."

Eitan sat back on his heels, considering. "Do you think Rand was, or is, Odile?"

"I considered it," Gideon said, then gestured to his head. "But you saw his face when I asked him." He shook his head. "No. I think he was telling the truth about that, at least. Espionage was a convenient lie to hang me with. I just don't know why."

"'You should never have touched her'," Eitan recalled Rand's last words. "Does he mean Msr Rand?"

"I don't know," Gideon said.

Eitan said nothing.

"Maybe," Gideon admitted, then cursed. "Probably. But it wasn't touching, touching, per se," he said. "It was more a heat-of-battle-we're-gonna-die touching. It . . . it felt like it might have been more," he continued, thinking back to that day in Fort Molina—the wet snow splatting over them as they hid, the burning wound in his arm, the pressure of the dispatch tube he'd liberated from an enemy officer digging into his ribs. Footsteps closing in and her eyes, so dark, so promising, that he'd come damn close to forgetting where they were and why . . .

Gideon shook his head. "It was pretty intense," he said. "But nothing actually happened, and even if it had—"

"Even if it had," Eitan cut in, "could Rand truly be so Earthbound he'd murder half a company and frame a man?"

"Believe me, I mean to ask," Gideon said. "But more, I mean to clear my name. The Twelfth Company's name."

Eitan, still crouched easily, nodded his understanding.

Gideon knew a sensitive reading took less time than talking, but still . . . "Don't your legs start to cramp up, sitting like that?"

"No," Eitan said, but then he rose and held his hand out.

Gideon accepted the lift, wavering only slightly on reaching his feet.

At the same time, the *Errant*'s engines sputtered to life, and Mia, Pitte, and Jinna came down the gangplank.

"Pratchett is one of my favorite classical writers." Pitte gestured at the book Mia clutched to her chest. "Next time we're in Nike, you can tell me what you think." Then he glanced at Jinna. "Though it may be awhile before we drop anchor at Nike."

"I really don't want to be any trouble," Jinna said with the air of someone continuing a previous discussion.

"So you've said," Pitte replied, confirming Gideon's supposition. "But lately, trouble is pretty much the *Errant*'s stock in trade."

As if on cue, the port aft engine sputtered, whined, and ground to silence.

"I'm on it!" Rory shouted from within.

"Really," Pitte said, "it always works out. Eventually."

"It'll be fine," Mia promised, giving Jinna a bolstering nudge.

"Sure," Jinna said.

"I'll take care of Del," Gideon heard himself say, then wondered where on toxic Earth that had come from.

"Oh, but—"

"It'll work out," he said, almost echoing Pitte's earlier promise, which made him look at Pitte, himself. "So, you're okay?"

"I've had worse," Pitte replied with a glance at Eitan before he added, "I should have taken care of Rand. I was going down for insubordination, anyway. I should have taken care of him."

"Not to worry," Gideon told him. "I will."

"Del *and* Rand?" Pitte's eyes narrowed. "That seems a tall order."

"Not for the commander of the Dirty Dozen," Eitan said.

Gideon's lips quirked, and he turned to his former second-in-command. "Do you want in on this?"

Eitan's eyes flickered with something cold and hard. "I wish I could," he said. "But I have obligations here." He glanced up at the *Errant*, then back to Gideon. "But please, feel free to give General Rand my regards."

"You can take that to the apiary," Gideon promised.

Then the port engine sparked to life, causing Elvis to jump from his perch on the gondola and land on Gideon's shoulder, where the need to soothe the draco's hissing displeasure prohibited any further discussion.

Soon after, the *Errant* lifted off, and Mia and Gideon were back in the borrowed Edsel, heading back to the city.

CHAPTER 15

MIA, SLOUCHED IN THE PASSENGER SEAT, TRIED TO ENJOY
her second actual ride in an auto, but the weight of John's novel
in her pocket reminded her she'd need to find a place to hide the
book from Ellison.

At which point she realized this was the first time she'd
given Ellison a thought since the fight at Kit's Diner.

"Problem?"

At the question, she looked at Gideon. He was eying the
road ahead, Elvis nestled around his shoulders like some scaly
version of a scarf.

"Just thinking." She shrugged. "You worked that business
with Jinna smooth as honey. Or you did until the . . ." Here, she
grabbed her throat and mock-throttled herself.

"Yeah well . . ." Now he shrugged and surprised her with a
look of genuine shame before he returned his eyes to the road.
"Lucky for all of us, cooler—and better-armed—heads
prevailed." He paused, tapped the steering wheel. "Anyway,
there wasn't much to work. It was more—facilitating Jinna's
move to a less stressful environment."

"Oooh, fancy talk," Mia grinned. "So when you were forking Rolf inna sausage n'beans, you was just—"

"*Were* just—"

"—facilitating him round to your point of view?"

He smiled. "Something like that."

It was a nice smile and completely at odds with the cold, deadly rage that had overtaken him when he'd first laid eyes on Captain Pitte.

Mia didn't think she'd ever been more scared than in that moment, or more confused when, after everything was done and dusted, both Gideon and John seemed to be getting on just fine.

Grown-ups, she thought—and not for the first time—were all a little swarm in the head.

And some, like old man Del and Fagin Ellison, were just plain mean.

But Gideon wasn't mean.

Angry, sure.

A body didn't need to be a sensitive to know there was an Earth-sized fury lurking under the twisty sense of humor. But even in their short acquaintance, Mia had never seen that anger aimed at someone who didn't deserve it.

Not even at herself, when he'd learned she meant to steal Elvis.

Which again reminded her of Ellison and what he was waiting for.

"Sure there's not a problem?" Gideon asked again.

"No," she said, then immediately added, "maybe."

He waited, eyes on the road, head tilted to show he was listening.

She sighed. "It's like this, then. Night's gettin' on, right? And it's great Jinna's settled, but . . ."

"But you're not," he filled in the silence. "Because of your fagin and Elvis."

"Yeah," she said, leaning back against the seat. "I'd be in comb and crystal if I could figure out how to facilitate Ellison."

To that, Gideon seemed to have no response, and they rode the rest of the way to the city in silence.

"You're counting again," Mia said, and Gideon promptly stopped counting; out loud, anyway.

It was close to 0200 hours, and they'd just dropped the Edsel off a few blocks from where Gideon had first found it.

The reason they didn't return the Comet to its original parking place was that the owner had apparently decided he wanted to take a late-night drive and discovered his ride was missing. All of which meant that, by the time Gideon cruised by on the cross street, the sidewalk was alive with lights, coppers, and concerned-slash-nosy neighbors.

"Oy, that's Detective Sergeant Hama," Mia had whispered, pointing to a man of medium height in plain clothes who appeared to be questioning the concerned-slash-nosy neighbors.

"You know the coppers by name?"

"A few," she said. "Hama's decent, for a copper," she continued, angling to see the detective. "Not on the take from anyone, high up or low down. If he was, Ellison would be doin' a lot more business in the ninth district."

Thankfully, the decent Hama was too busy to look in their direction, so Gideon drove on, not stopping for another couple blocks before leaving the car near the ninth district's police station.

Though in unfamiliar territory, Mia assured Gideon they were only a few streets away from the Elysium Inn and Shakespeare Circus, but where the Circus and lodging were in wide, well-lit regions, the streets they walked now were darker and barely wide enough for a rickshaw.

They were also crowded, the streets teeming with laborers looking for a good time in the cramped pubs lining the way.

Some, seeming to want more than a pint, could be seen passing starbucks to nondescript characters loitering on various stoops in exchange for small packets.

"I can see why they call Nike the city that never sleeps," Gideon said as he dodged a trio linked either in a torrid embrace or a three-way wrestling match.

"Late drinkers make good marks," Mia said, trotting along at his side.

"Tell me you have not been dipping your way from the cop shop," Gideon said, then came to a standstill so quickly that Elvis, dozing on his shoulder, almost fell off, and Mia took a few more steps before she realized he was no longer moving.

"What is it?" she asked, turning back.

"Speaking of cops, isn't that your Detective Sergeant Hama? From the Edsel?" He jerked his chin to a nearby corner, where the man with dark skin and a lightly graying beard they'd spied less than an hour ago was in conversation with a rumpled civilian.

"That's him," Mia agreed, following Gideon as he joined the queue outside a pub bearing the ponderous name of The Old Man and the Sea.

"Do you know the woman he's talking to?" Gideon asked.

"A dealer," she said. "Goes by Dr. Bayer, but I don't think she's really a doctor."

Gideon would bet his last few starbucks that Mia was right. "You're not a client, are you?"

"Nah, but Ellison is," she said with obvious distaste while Gideon watched Bayer put on a show—and it was clearly a show—of the put-upon "just an honest businesswoman" routine.

Hama, his bearded face still revealing an expression of blatant disbelief, was in fact listening closely, nodding on occasion as Bayer's story wound on.

When at last she stopped talking, he grimaced, then made a slick pass from his pocket to her hand before delivering a textbook admonishment to clear off the street or face the consequences.

Gideon continued to watch as the woman departed, suitably chastised. "Wonder what she sold him?"

"No drugs," Mia said. "I told you, Hama's a decent sort. Probably she sold 'im another dealer."

"Maybe." Then as Hama turned in their direction, Gideon ducked behind a man with hair as curly as Mia's, dressed in a riverman's oilskin coat.

"Why are we hiding?" Mia whispered, offering a grin to a pair of women in burn-spattered coveralls.

"I don't know," Gideon confessed, also quietly. "Just a feeling." He peered through the riverman's bobbing curls to see Hama staring in their general direction.

The riverman turned around, and Gideon shifted to stay out of Hama's line of sight.

"You'd best not be angling for my purse," the man said, the warm Dole accent a direct contrast to the chill of his frown.

"S'okay," Mia told the man quickly. "We're just duckin' the filth."

"Law on your back, my friend?" The riverman's eyes crinkled.

"They might be," Gideon said, shooting Mia a look.

"No problem here." The riverman held up his right hand to show the faded prison tattoo. "That your man?" he asked the general air around himself. "In the bad suit?"

"That's him," Mia said, peering around the coat.

"He still looking around," their new best friend told them,

angling about as if waiting for someone. "Uniform just joined him. She got her notebook in her hand. They talking and . . . it's all good. Your man and his officer are moving on to Beam Street."

Gideon leaned around to confirm, and it seemed DS Hama had indeed disappeared. "Thanks."

"Anytime," the riverman said. "And friend . . ." He waited for Gideon to turn back. "You decide you want to take sail from your troubles, the *Amber Queen* ships out tomorrow night, pier sixteen. Just ask for Juban."

"Yeah. I mean, no. I mean thanks, but—never mind." Gideon waved off the grinning sailor and, with Mia, headed out into the street.

Mia took one look at him and shook her head. "Come on," she said, grabbing Gideon's hand and tugging him onwards. "This way."

"Where are we going now?"

"Somewhere you can get some rest. You're knackered."

"I dunno, I had a nice little nap after Jagati clocked me."

Her gaze slid sideways. "You had that coming."

Gideon ran a hand over the lump on his skull. "I absolutely did."

While Gideon and Mia were ducking the filth, inside The Old Man and the Sea, Freya Ohmdahl and her brothers were catching up with Rey and Ronan Pradesh.

Though the Ohmdahls and Pradeshes were acquainted— siblings in the freelance muscle business were bound to run across one another—the twins weren't known for social drinking.

Or, for that matter, socializing in general.

Freya's surprise at seeing the twins in the pub quickly turned to curiosity when, on greeting Rey, she discovered the pair were scouring the district for a man who sounded a lot like the soldier who had trounced Freya and her brothers earlier that night.

It was then, in solidarity with another family suffering through the post-war job crisis, that Ulf and Rolf happily described the man who'd put the wasp in the hive of their own job.

"Though Miss Jinna got Ulf pretty good with that mustard," Rolf concluded.

"Almost as good as that dodger got you wid dat teapot," Ulf countered, grinning over his swollen nose.

But Rey was focused on the soldier. "Blue eyes, you say? And tall?"

"Skinny too," Freya confirmed, tossing back a shot of vodka that Gideon had paid for. "I am thinking he could use some of Mama's kugel."

Rey smiled at that, but not the laughing kind of smile, before asking if Freya and her brothers would be willing to show them where they'd last seen Gideon, which was why the Ohmdahls and Pradeshes were exiting the pub only a few moments after Gideon and Mia turned down the street.

"Look at that." Rolf pointed his sausage-like finger at Gideon's retreating back. "That is the fellow we told of, the one with Mia the dodger."

"I will be limping for a week because of dat man," Ulf added.

"He is a good fighter," Freya noted with respect. "And not snooty, like Del. Him, we will not work for again. *Wait!*" she called to Rey, who had already taken off after the soldier, Ronan on her heels.

Ulf looked at Rolf, who looked at Freya, who shrugged, and then all three took off, much less fluidly, after the twins.

If nothing else, Freya figured they would have the chance to thank Gideon for the drinks.

CHAPTER 16

He knew they were being followed because if they weren't, all the shouts of protest, grunts of pain, and crashes of glass breaking behind them were the beginnings of Nike's most specifically transient bar fight ever.

He hoped just this once his instincts were off, and the noise really was the result of a pub brawl-crawl, but a quick glance over his shoulder showed him five figures—two slim and dark and three broad and fair—plowing through the street. "Uh oh."

Mia glanced over. "That sounds bad."

"It is. The triplets are coming." He turned and gave Mia a *let's hurry* hand on her shoulder. "With their friends, the mercenary twins."

"What twins?" she asked, but hurriedly in deference to the hand.

"Remember the woman from the alley?"

"The one with the slithery voice." Mia pulled him left, off of Marlboro and onto a still smaller street, one of those formed when more buildings were erected than the original city plan allowed for.

"That one, yes. Her name is Rey."

"She was pissed—"

"Angry."

"—that you bashed her brother. You never mentioned they was twins."

"*Were* twins, and it didn't seem relevant at the time."

Mia, no surprise, rolled her eyes. Then she took a sharp right into a narrow walkway.

Gideon squeezed her shoulder to stop, and both flattened against the building as he leaned out to see what was happening behind them while Elvis craned his neck up and out as well.

At first, Gideon thought they'd lost the full hive of siblings, but a flurry of motion at the corner of Marlboro told him they were still coming.

"Time to scarp," he said.

Mia nodded and led the way deeper into a passage made up of buildings so old and ramshackle, he suspected they only remained upright by leaning against each other.

He also found it odd that the entrances were all below street level, so one had to descend a staircase to get to the front door. He was going to ask about the odd feature when he got a whiff of ease-laced smoke through a cracked window and the question turned into a cough.

By the time he could breathe again, Mia swung left, down a set of stairs to one of the sub-level doors.

Gideon followed, less enthusiastically. "Tell me this isn't your someplace quiet."

"Nah, this is just a shortcut."

Gideon, still on the steps, could smell the teasing edges of ease, trip, and who knew what other narcotics. He glanced back into the narrow lane. "So far, so good. Maybe we've lost—"

And then an Ohmdahl-like shout was followed by a Ronan-like shadow, and he knew they were out of time.

"Never mind." He ducked into the house, and Mia followed, closing the door behind them.

He reached back to lock the door, but Mia shook her head. "If they're trying the doors, and one's locked . . ."

"It'll look like someone's hiding something." He nodded, then coughed again as the smoke that had only teased its way past the door hung thickly in the house itself.

It stung Gideon's eyes, rasped in his throat, clouded his senses, and infuriated Elvis, who set his wings to flapping the pernicious substance away.

"Thanks," Gideon told him.

Through the haze, he could just make out a long central hall with an ascending stairway facing the entrance and rooms opening on either side. All, he assumed, occupied by whoever was making all that smoke.

Mia didn't hesitate and headed straight through, past the stairs and the rooms, into the kitchen and then right to another door.

"Now where?" Gideon rasped.

Mia, holding one sleeve-covered hand over her nose and mouth, opened the door with the other to show a set of stairs leading down.

Bad idea, Gideon thought.

Then he heard the front door beginning to creak open behind them.

They went downstairs.

The lower area was as large as the upper floor, but divided by a series of free-standing screens, and while there was enough smoke to calm an acre of bees, it was of the lighter, less narcotic variety found in pubs and hookah shops.

Gideon had never thought of tobacco as particularly refreshing, but in comparison to what was being inhaled upstairs, the basement was like a walk through a spring shower.

"This way," Mia said again, leading him through the forest of screens.

As they moved, the air became less fuggy, and Gideon was even able to blink away some of the tears to see an open window.

An open window in the basement.

He looked at Mia, his eyes questioning.

"Wolstonecroft Street," she said softly and pointed to where the window was set next to a crookedly hung door. "It's a full story lower than Byron."

From upstairs, the sound of heavy footsteps shook the ceiling. Mia, still filtering the air through her sleeve, tugged him past a meadow of reclining individuals, all sharing an apiary's worth of water pipes, before hitting another narrow hall which led to the basement exit.

"Wait," Gideon said quickly, grabbing Mia's hand as she reached for the door's handle.

A feeling was growing in the pit of his stomach—the same sort he'd feel when a mission was about to go swarm—meaning either he was suffering from a contact high, or . . .

He studied the door, top to bottom, then with a speed that belied the fug in his brains, slammed the door's rusty lock home.

"*What?*" Mia hissed as he took her by the arm and dragged her along back through the hall, then down another short corridor that branched away from the somnolent party. "What're you doing? We were almost home free."

"Crack under the door," he explained shortly as boots clumped heavily down the stairs. "The gap was big enough to see two pairs of boots waiting on the other side. Here." He stopped at the end of the hall, in front of a curtained-off section of wall.

The odor emanating from behind that curtain was about as far from a spring shower as he could imagine.

"Here, what?"

"Here is where you're going to hide," he said, pulling the curtain aside and immediately wishing he hadn't.

The curtain really did cut down on the privy's smell.

"Are you swarm?" she asked, almost choking on the odor. "We can't all fit in here—and those who do are like to suffocate."

"It's not that bad," he said. Actually, it was pretty bad. But behind him, whoever had come downstairs was rousing the torpid smokers from their respective stupors.

And now, someone was banging on the back door.

Gideon looked at Mia. "There's room for the two of you."

"Wait!" Her eyes went wide, making her, for once, seem as young as she actually was.

"Can't," he said, then straightened his arm and clicked his tongue to Elvis, who flowed from Gideon's shoulder to his wrist and then, when Gideon gave the sign, to Mia's shoulder. "Friend," he said to the draco. "Guard." And while Elvis showed his displeasure by shifting from leg to leg, he remained in place, his right forepaw resting in Mia's hair.

"No," she whispered, as if the draco hadn't been her sole desire at the beginning of the night. "We'll fight 'em. Like we did before."

"Can't," he said again. He crouched down quickly because, to his horror, the girl was actually near to tears. "The thing is, these aren't going to be the last. The person who sent the twins—"

"*Rand,*" she breathed the name.

"Yes, Rand," Gideon agreed as a rush of fresh air from behind told him the basement door was now open. "Rand's like Killian Del. He has money and power, and even if we could fight them all—and we can't—Rand won't stop sending people after me."

"But—"

"They're not looking for *you*. And I'd like to keep it that way."

Her face began to crumple, and his heart seemed to be going along for the ride.

Must be something in the smoke . . .

Footsteps were closing in. The screens Mia had led him around were being torn aside, or simply through.

"Keep Elvis safe for me," he said. Then he rose and dropped the curtain before her expression could completely undo him, turned, and stepped out of the alcove where the five—no, *six*—pursuers waited.

Gideon frowned, then counted.

Three Ohmdahls, check.

Two angry twins, check.

And one—

"I'm sorry," he said to the sixth person, a smaller man with a distinguished mustache and wearing what looked to be a servant's uniform. "Who are you?"

"My name is Nahmin Soor," the small man said. "A pleasure to meet you, Colonel Quinn."

"Not colonel," Gideon said.

"As you wish."

Gideon stepped forward, trying to move the scene farther from Mia's hiding place. "Where did you come from?" he asked Nahmin.

"I found him waiting at the back door," Freya said, peering somewhat owlishly at the small man. "First I wonder, 'who is this little man pounding on the door, and why is he also looking for Gideon?' but then I think, the more the happier, yes?"

"No," Gideon said, glancing at the six standing between him and any hope of freedom, "not really."

"That's just hurtful," Nahmin said, looking past Gideon's shoulder.

"Did you bring the carriage?" Rey asked.

"It is just outside," Nahmin replied.

"I thought you were looking for a higher class of employer," Gideon said to the Ohmdahls.

"You've met one another?" Nahmin asked Gideon.

"I facilitated an understanding between the triplets and a young lady."

"Nice girl," Rolf agreed. "Friend of Mia the dodger."

"Small world," Nahmin observed.

"Gideon even gave us some starbucks, for our troubles," Ulf tossed in.

"Well," Gideon replied, "I did cost you a job, so—"

"Enough!" Ronan cut Gideon off with a shove that sent him stumbling toward the privy curtain. He barely avoided crashing through it by twisting wildly and grabbing hold of Rey's sleeve, which went about as well as one could expect.

"Ow," he said, rubbing at the side of his head—at least she hadn't hit the same spot as Jagati—while noting that the Ohmdahl triplets were beginning to look less cheerful.

Nahmin must have noticed as well, as he turned to face the three giants. "Thank you for your assistance," he told them. "But we can take over from here."

The Ohmdahls, however, were not eager to shuffle off the stage. "We are happy to help," Freya said, while her brothers both nodded.

"A generous offer," Nahmin replied, "but our business with Msr Quinn is just that—business—and dull business at that. There will be no need for your particular skill set."

And as the butler-like man spoke, Gideon saw him flick a stiletto into his hand, angling it so only Gideon could see the gleaming blade. "I'm sure Msr Quinn wouldn't want to keep you from your pleasures. Would he?" He turned to Rey and Ronan, both armed, then gestured at the privy curtain, leaving no doubt just how messy things could get should Gideon contradict him.

"Absolutely not," Gideon replied, meeting the small man's dark gaze before turning to the triplets. "You should all go, get home to your mom."

"You are certain?" Freya asked.

"Very," Gideon said.

"You see? Everything is honey in the comb here." Nahmin smiled and, to Gideon's relief, the triplets finally accepted the dismissal.

Still, Nahmin's blade remained low and ready, and not until the Ohmdahls were well on their way through the rumpled pallets, pillows, and screens did he turn his attention back to Gideon. "Now, if you don't mind, the carriage is waiting."

"Wait." Rey held up a hand.

"For what?" Nahmin asked as Rey produced a length of rope.

"This," Ronan said, before delivering a punch that landed firmly in Gideon's kidney.

Mia, who'd remained as close to frozen as she'd ever been, waited until the sounds of footsteps faded to a safe distance before daring to peek through the heavy curtains.

The angle wasn't good, but she could see Gideon, his hands bound behind him, being escorted in the direction of the Wolstonecroft door between a man and a woman who had to be the twins.

Coming up behind was the little man she'd first spied close to eight hours and half a lifetime ago, following Gideon. This time the chameleon of a poisoner was dressed in the togs of a high-end servant.

Just as he was about to round the corner, the little man turned in Mia's direction and, even though she knew he couldn't possibly see her through the sliver of space between the curtains, she watched him once again raise his index finger and shake it back and forth in warning, exactly as he had when she'd spied him outside the Elysium earlier that night.

He held the position for a beat, then turned away and continued on after Gideon and the others, leaving Mia with the revelation that there were people way scarier than Ellison.

Elvis must have been worried as well, because for the first time since she'd laid eyes on the draco, he'd not moved so much as a talon while his person headed into what looked to be some pretty deep fertilizer.

"But we're not gonna leave him in it, are we?" she asked the draco, still perched on her shoulder.

Elvis apparently knew she was addressing him, because his neck snaked around so they were eye to eye, and his head shook in what appeared to be both echo and denial of Nahmin's forbidding finger.

Moments later, Mia and Elvis were outside.

Wolstonecroft street was empty but for the echo of a carriage and four rattling over the cobbles that made up most of the streets in this district.

"If you can find 'im, I'll keep up," Mia said to Elvis.

Again, the draco proved himself keener than most people Mia knew as, rumbling low in his throat, he launched himself from her shoulder, taking flight above the rickety housetops and flying in the same direction as the receding clomp of hooves.

"Wicked," Mia judged, then raced after the draco, using the routes known only to the dodgers of Fagin Ellison.

It didn't occur to her, at the time, that it was Fagin Ellison who'd first mapped out those routes.

Ronan shoved Gideon into the narrow street to discover the same carriage that had pulled up to the Elysium waiting.

Which was all Gideon had time to notice before a sack was yanked over his head from behind.

"Nice," he muttered, even as he was roughly guided up the steps and into the carriage interior, which felt as spacious on the inside as it appeared on the outside.

Then he was being shoved onto a cushioned bench, and two bodies bounced to either side, bracketing him.

Though the burlap left him blind, Gideon could hear the shift of a body on the opposite bench.

He suspected it was Rand but didn't have time to address the other passenger as, the second the carriage began to roll, the first punch struck, knocking his head sideways and splitting open his cheek.

From there, the pummeling continued from both sides. Gideon, slumping to the floor, tried to remind himself it could be worse.

It had been worse a time or two in his life, like when he'd ended up in the hands of that Midasian interrogator, or facing off with Renny Boucher in that vein in the Barrens . . . or when he'd been aboard the *Kodiak*, facing Rand from the inside of a cage.

Over the rush of internal static accompanying another boot to the kidney, he thought he heard a word, and that word might have been "enough," and perhaps it was since the attacks ceased as suddenly as they'd begun.

Curled on the rumbling floor of the carriage, Gideon remained tense as he breathed in the odor of blood, burlap, leather, and—oddly—an undercurrent of something spicy and subtle that tickled the edges of his memory.

Rather than dwell on the pain, his thoughts danced over those muffled scents, latching on to leather, which in Gideon's experience meant boots shined to gleaming, the scabbard of his sword, the strap of a rifle, that interrogator's whip . . . and the interior of this very fine carriage, he thought, sliding closer to the present.

"Suede," the ghost of Dani's voice whispered through the fog. Her long fingers brushed cool against the broken skin over his cheekbone, drawing Gideon back, back to the past . . . to when she was his. "Blue suede shoes."

"You never wore blue suede shoes," he told her.

"No," she agreed, leaning close to brush her lips over his as she added, "I never wore perfume, either."

Which was when he remembered.

Perfume.

Spicy.

Subtle.

Celia.

CHAPTER 17

Fort Molina
Eastern Allianza Border
October 17, 1442 After Landing

WET SNOW PATTERED OVER THE REMAINS OF THE STILL-smoking fort, misting the air and, hopefully, masking Celia Rand's squeal as the soldier Gideon had just killed dropped to the muddy ground.

While the majority of Gideon's company were off-base, guarding their transpo, Gideon, Nbo, and Eitan had split up in search of Msr Rand, the better to avoid the scatter of enemy soldiers patrolling the decimated fort.

Which, in itself Gideon thought odd.

Why bother taking the fort and then leaving it with only the barest guard? A question second only to that of how a general's spouse had managed to miss the fort's evac.

A wet splat of snow slid down Gideon's neck, reminding him he could fixate on those questions at a later date.

Right now he had to get Msr Rand—and her bright red coat—out of sight.

While wet snow steamed from the body of the fallen Midasian, Gideon dragged the sputtering woman into the wreckage of Fort Molina's mess hall.

His right arm was burned and bleeding, his rifle was slagged, and his knife was lodged in the throat of that unfortunate Midasian corpsman.

"Do you mind?" Msr Rand hissed, whipping her arm free of his grip.

"You're welcome," he muttered, ignoring the burning in his arm as he assessed the damage to his rifle.

Deciding it was best used as a club at this point, he positioned himself next to a blasted-out gap in the wall and listened for sounds of any further enemy activity.

A soft shuffle of fabric had him turning to find the woman whipping off her scarf, which she proceeded to wrap around his wound. "Stay back," he whispered. "Anyone sees a hint of that coat, we're done."

"What's wrong with my coat?" she whispered back, tightening the knot, hard.

Gideon gritted his teeth. "Nothing, except it's visible from a few hundred meters."

"No one would have had the chance to *see* my coat if you hadn't wasted so much time searching that officer you killed." Her words were barely more than a breath tickling his ears.

Gideon inhaled a breath of her perfume and exhaled it slowly, suddenly hyper-aware of the woman at his side. "The search was S.O.P.—standard operating procedure," he explained quietly, while also confirming he still carried the dispatches taken from the enemy officer.

"Of course," she murmured after a beat, then added a barely audible, "I'm sorry."

The words were short, quiet, and tugged at Gideon in a way they had no right to.

In a way, in fact, that had him turning to see her deep brown eyes filling with tears. He suddenly realized that, wife of a general or no, this woman had been through an ordeal.

He could now, all too clearly, imagine the terror of two days on her own before a Midasian officer discovered her, followed by the shock of Gideon's arrival, and subsequent killing of said officer.

"You'll be all right," he murmured, clearing his throat as she pressed close, trembling against him, snow melting on the midnight of her hair. "I promise, you're going to get out of here."

"I believe—" she began but stopped as the crunch of footsteps in icy mud cut through the plop of wet snow.

Gideon moved her against the wall, pressing her back and holding a finger to his lips. She nodded, eyes wide, her pulse fluttering visibly as her lips parted.

For a mad second, Gideon was tempted to take those lips— and anything else on offer.

Cursing inwardly, he eased away, leaving the woman to follow along with the footsteps on the other side of the wall.

He paused next to the opening as the footsteps came to a halt near the open frame of what had been the door. He held his breath, preparing to engage whatever came through that door, but before he got there, another Midasian burst from behind a pile of what had been the mess's roof.

Gideon spun towards the new threat and found himself face to face with a fully charged crysto-plas rifle.

Shit, he thought, but when the blast came, it wasn't Gideon who fell, but the Midasian.

He watched the enemy drop to her knees, her eyes wide, her expression shocked, to reveal Celia Rand standing behind her, both hands gripping the smallest shooter he'd ever seen.

And where had she been hiding that? he wondered.

"Sir?" Nbo's voice had Gideon spinning again, this time to see his sergeant leaning through the opening. "Ready to go?"

He stared, then shook his head, then turned and crossed to where Celia still stood, staring down at the woman she'd killed. "It's okay," he said, pressing the shooter down. "You're okay."

At which point Celia looked up at him, her expression suddenly as cold as the snow falling outside. "Are we leaving now?"

CHAPTER 18

THE COACH LURCHED TO A HALT, LITERALLY KNOCKING Gideon free of the memory, but he said nothing, only waited as the horses stamped and the door opened, letting in a blast of chill air.

Rough hands hauled him up, then maneuvered him out and down the carriage steps.

Only when he heard the rustle of fabric and caught a fresh waft of perfume did he speak. "Celia," he croaked, then cleared his throat. "It's been a while."

"And yet," the reply came after a beat, "not long enough."

Then the sack was whipped away, and for the first time in almost seven years, Gideon laid eyes on Celia Rand. Her hair was shorter, he noted, but she was still wearing red.

"Nahmin." Celia glanced at the man climbing down from the coachman's perch. "Take care of the horses, then see that the general remains undisturbed." She looked at the twins. "Bring him. And Gideon . . ." She paused, looked back over her shoulder. "Try not to bleed on the carpet."

"Ha ha," Gideon said, then grunted as the twins propelled

him into the house, up the stairs and down the hall in Celia's wake before shoving him into the last room on the second floor.

Within seconds of Gideon's entrance, Celia had stepped out of her shoes. Then as he watched, bemused, she began to move about the room, lighting a series of table lamps.

Pockets of illumination grew to fill the space, revealing burgundy flocked wallpaper, red velvet curtains framing long windows, and furniture that ran to the fancy: a gilded wardrobe, delicately carved tables and chairs, a curved divan, and a fireplace mantle crowded with antiquities—including a collection of Earth-made soda bottles.

Even the bed was a showcase, with its sea of red satin nesting inside an ebony frame.

He turned to see Celia had lit the final lamp and was closing the thick curtains, possibly worried the neighbors might wake up and spy the strange man bleeding all over the brocade.

With the curtains closed, she walked to a small table holding a decanter and several glasses, unstoppered the decanter and poured out a glass of burgundy-tinted liquid.

Holding his gaze, Celia lifted the glass, sampled it, and smiled her approval.

"One hates to ask," Gideon said, studying her, "but why am I not floating face-down in the Avon with your husband's knife in my back?"

"That is a question," she murmured.

Gideon frowned as the use of that particular phrase set an itch to the back of his brain.

Before he could scratch it, Rey nudged him into one of the chairs, a burgundy-cushioned number with an ornately carved slat back. Ronan joined them to bind Gideon's hands to the chair rails.

He waited for the twins to move away, then counted to ten

before beginning to test the bindings, slowly flexing and stretching his wrists before his hands, already numb, lost all function, turned black, and fell off, rendering any escape attempt moot.

Aren't you being a little overdramatic? he asked himself.

Have you seen where we are? His self replied, eyes remaining on Celia while she set down the glass and shed her coat, revealing a blood red gown that didn't so much cling to her curves as promise to, pausing over various bits of anatomy until a turn, a step, a twist, caused it to ripple away and on to new territory.

As far as Gideon could tell, there was nothing holding the gown in place but a slender strap over one shoulder, and that strap was little more than a prayer away from releasing its tenuous hold.

"Um," Gideon said.

"A moment." Celia draped the coat over the back of the divan, then looked at the twins. "You may wait in the hall for Nahmin's signal."

Signal? Gideon wondered. He remained silent until the door closed behind the twins, then looked at Celia. "Signal?" he asked.

"I imagine you're thirsty," she said, retrieving her glass.

Gideon spat a gob of bloody saliva onto the rug. "I could drink."

Her mouth quirked, a shadow of a smile, as she joined him and held the glass to his lips.

He inhaled the scent of raspberries and alcohol, which mingled seductively with the spice of her perfume.

With his eyes locked on hers, he took a swallow, then another, and another until she withdrew the goblet and brushed her fingers over his lower lip, bringing a stray drop of the liquid to her tongue, much as Doc had done with a drop of sweat in the Morton yard only days before.

"You kept the coat," she noted. "Interesting."

"Why?"

"Because keeping it says you don't blame the Corps for what happened to you."

"Why would I blame the Corps for something your husband did?"

Celia's shoulder lifted in a tiny shrug. "Not everyone would have such a clear view of the matter."

"Not that clear," Gideon muttered, still worrying at the rope. "For instance, why did your husband believe we had an affair?"

"Oh, Jessup never believed we had an affair."

You should never have touched her . . . Rand's last words in the *Kodiak*'s brig seemed to echo in the over-warm room. "Then . . ."

"He believes you assaulted me in Allianza."

"And why," Gideon asked, though his voice was tight, "would he think that?"

"Because that's what I told him."

"*You* told him?" Gideon forced the question through the rage clogging his throat. "And he believed you?"

Celia's gaze remained cool as she studied him. "I had some very impressive bruises to show as proof. You were quite the brute."

Gideon's wrists wrenched so violently that the skin tore. "*Why?*"

"You appear quite fit for someone who's been living on prison rations," she said, ignoring the question of the day. "That said," her fingers brushed over his bruised cheek, "you also look like someone has been using you for target practice."

The salve of her voice crashed into Gideon's fury, leaving

him still angry, but also dizzy. "Several someones have," he managed.

"Poor Gideon." She tilted his chin up and pressed her lips to the pulse point under his jaw, causing his blood to heat.

He closed his eyes, willing himself not to respond.

"Interesting," she murmured, and suddenly he was deeply aware of her absence.

Opening his eyes, he watched Celia cross to the table where she'd left the liqueur. Her back was turned, but he heard the clink of crystal as she unstoppered the decanter. "What's interesting?" he asked.

"Your self-control," she replied as she poured. "It's stronger than it was at Allianza, and it was impressive then." She turned, holding a full glass, and met his gaze. "You're staring, Colonel."

"What can I say?" He managed an indolent shrug. "Seven years hasn't made you less of a walking heart attack."

"I'll take that as a compliment," she decided.

"Don't," he said and was surprised by the flash of hurt in her eyes, though the shift of expression was so swift, he couldn't be certain.

"Do you know," she began, staring in her turn, "you are the only one who's ever said no to me and meant it?"

Which was not something he expected to hear. "Ah—"

"Generals, diplomats, the ever-present servants, every single one of my assets fell for my charms. Willingly. Happily. Every one of them." She paused and looked into the red depths of the glass, then up, again meeting his gaze. "Until you."

Which, Gideon thought, was wrong.

Not that he didn't believe her claims of conquest. He pretty much hated Celia's silk-wrapped guts, but he still wanted her.

No, what was wrong was the other bit, the thing about the, "Assets," he repeated.

Rather than respond, she set the glass on the long, low table in front of the chaise, exchanging it for one of the knickknacks littering its surface.

It was, he noted distantly, a music box. One she wound now so when she set it back in its place, it began to play.

"I've always loved this piece," she told him, taking up the goblet.

Then, to his jaw dropping wonder, Celia began to dance; rising lightly on her bare feet, she extended a leg here, an arm there, before spinning her way across the room with such ease that not a drop of the deep red liqueur spilled from the glass.

Gideon was near to breathless by the time she came to a stop in front of him, at which point every cogent thought rushed out of his brain.

"Do you like it?" she asked, and though Gideon didn't know if she meant the music, the dance, or her, his head dropped in a single truncated nod, then his breath caught as she folded herself onto his lap.

"Do you know where this music came from?" she asked, leaning close, her berry-scented breath tickling his ear.

"No."

"It's very old," she told him, easing back as she explained. "It was old even when our ancestors left Earth." She slid one arm behind his neck. "It was part of a ballet." As she spoke, she lifted the goblet to his lips and tipped the glass so Gideon automatically drank from it, though the berry-scented wine did nothing to ease the tightness in his throat.

"This particular music is a movement from a ballet called *Swan Lake*," she continued, lowering the glass, now barely half-full. "The 'Black Swan Pas de Deux,' it's called."

Gideon licked the traces of liqueur from his lips, which felt suddenly hot. "It was stunning," he said, then flushed at the naked admiration in that statement.

"I know," she said, pressing her forehead to his, and he couldn't tell but thought her voice hinted at sadness.

"Celia," he began as a fresh welling of regret surfaced from —somewhere.

"That black swan has a name," she cut in, her voice almost as choked as his as she straightened, her expression becoming distant even as the storm of need and sorrow swamping Gideon receded like the tide. "Do you want to know it?"

He wasn't sure he did.

"Her name," Celia continued, her gaze steady, "is Odile."

"Odile," he echoed, the Midasian code name for which he'd gone to prison falling numbly from his lips.

"Yes," she said, still watching him.

"But . . . you saved my life in Allianza," he said. "You killed that Midasian soldier."

"I killed that Midasian soldier," she said, "because your sergeant entered the mess. I had to protect my cover."

"That is . . . cold," was the best he could manage.

"That is war," she corrected. "Though I suppose I should thank you properly for taking the fall on my behalf."

"Untie these ropes," he suggested. "We'll work something out."

"I don't think so." She traced a finger over his collarbone. "But maybe, before it's all finished, I'll have the chance to make it up to you." And then she leaned close, brushing her lips over the same spot her finger had traced seconds before.

It wasn't much—the faintest touch—but it was still enough to send Gideon's entire system into overdrive.

"Stop," he said, clenching his teeth against the unwanted desire.

"You don't really want me to stop," Celia murmured, dark eyes peering up.

"Yes, I do," he hissed, hating that he was lying and hating even more that she *knew* he was lying.

It was in that moment, when fury and desire declared war on each other, that his arms jerked backwards and the chair's finely carved slats snapped and he surged out of the chair, knocking Celia to the carpet and sending the glass flying from her hand.

He didn't have his hands—the original binding still held—but he was bigger than her, stronger than her, and he was sure as toxic Earth madder than her, so when she fell, he followed, setting one knee over her throat and pressing so there was only a thin trickle of air between Celia and the death of a swan.

It was tempting, so very tempting, to remain where he was.

To end it.

To end her.

Except for the unfortunate truth—a truth Gideon, even half-mad with rage, could recognize—that the only thing Celia's death would end was his freedom.

And her, Gideon reminded himself.

Again, tempting.

But not, in the end, tempting enough.

He removed the knee and sank back on his heels, and it was a good thing he did, because as the hot fuel of rage receded, so too went the energy that had propelled him from the chair in the first place.

"Thank you," Celia whispered hoarsely, drawing his attention to the bruise blossoming over her pale, pale throat.

"I'm not the murderer in this room," he said with some difficulty. He must be more exhausted than he thought. Either that or—

"Not yet," she said, interrupting his train of thought.

"I . . . what?" Keepers, but he was tired all of a sudden. And now there were the shadows spilling over the edges of his vision, much as the liqueur had spilled over the carpet.

The liqueur, he thought, looking to the fallen goblet and remembering that, though Celia had drunk from the first serving, she hadn't touched a drop of the second.

Hells, he thought, slumping to one side as the morph numbed his limbs for the second time that night.

He figured it was probably the drug talking as well, when he heard Celia's soft, *"I'm sorry."*

CHAPTER 19

"C'MON, C'MON, C'MON," MIA MUTTERED AS SHE SLID through a gap in a fence, leaving a scrap of her trousers, and darted through someone's handkerchief-sized garden.

It was only one of the obstacles she'd had to slide through, climb over, under, or avoid while following the draco that was trailing the carriage Gideon had been forced into.

Though, even as she did her best to keep up with Elvis, Mia wondered if the draco was really flying after Gideon, or if he was simply on his way to the nearest fishmonger for an early breakfast.

But then she glanced up to see Elvis circling back—as if to confirm she was, in fact, following—before striking off once more toward the city center, where the rich and powerful of the city dwelt.

Since there wasn't much in the way of fish stalls in the risto neighborhoods, Mia took heart and put on some speed.

Nearing the familiar territory of the Circus, she ducked low and sidled through a gap in the next fence, which brought her to Carroll Square, where the Elysium Inn looked out over the agri-center and wind farm.

She turned to look at the hotel, most of the windows dark by now.

From above, a high, keening call drew her attention skywards where the draco urged her onwards.

"I'm comin', I'm comin'," she muttered, picking up speed so that when she reached the gap in the agri-center's boundary hedge, she fair dove through the opening.

And came up short against the bulk that was Ellison.

"Figgered you might make a stop 'ere abouts," the fagin said, grabbing her arm. "I expected you a mite sooner, and wif a draco under your tunic," he growled as his hand tightened around her arm, hard enough that Mia had to bite down the protest. "I always knew you was trouble, but I never figured you for bein' disloyal."

"Let go o' me," she cried, trying to peel Ellison's white-knuckled fingers from around her biceps. "Let go or . . . or I'll lose it!"

"Lose it?" Ellison ignored the young dodger's struggles and hauled her up high enough she got a face full of whiskey-tinged breath when he asked, "Lose *what*?"

At which point a shrieking draco dove at Ellison, causing him to drop Mia in order to protect his bald head from the screaming, flapping Elvis.

"That," Mia said, springing to her feet and racing away from the cowering fagin.

Once she was well away, Elvis gave one last remonstrative shriek before swooping up and into the night after her.

Ellison, his blood running cold, remained where he was, hunched over between the winter wheat and the remains of last fall's tomato plants for many minutes, until he was convinced the demon with wings wasn't going to come at him again.

Eventually, when it became clear no further claws would come to tear at his exposed flesh, he slowly lowered his arm to find that, yes, he was alone.

Or rather, mostly alone.

Just on the far side of the tomato patch, a man of stocky build, wearing the keeper colors of saffron and crimson and carrying a hoe with the same assurance a soldier carries his sword, stood staring. "Might one ask," the keeper began, his basso voice deceptively pleasant, "what in the comb you'd be doing in my wheat in the wee hours?"

"I . . ." Ellison's eyes darted wildly to the sky and then around him, then to the sky again. "Did you see it?"

The keeper's eyes widened, and he hefted the hoe suggestively. "See what?"

As he spoke, two other keepers—a woman of middle years and a youth—came racing up to join the first keeper.

"We telephed the precinct," the youth said. "They'll be sending someone along, quick as they can."

"They also said it may be awhile." The woman turned her disapproving eyes on Ellison. "They say it's a busy night."

"That's fine, that is," the first keeper said. "It'll give our friend here time to settle and explain himself in proper fashion." His weighty gaze fixed on Ellison. "Won't it?"

"It . . . I . . . Yes," Ellison replied at last, still hunching in on himself.

On the whole, Ellison was accustomed to confrontations with people under the age of fourteen; when it came to facing off with adults, he generally found cowardice to be the better part of valor.

Or, in this instance, cowardice and bald-faced lies.

Lies produced for the keepers and reiterated on the arrival

of the coppers, in which he claimed himself a victim of thieves who set upon him as he stepped out of his favorite tavern.

Afraid for his life, he'd run roughshod through the streets until he'd finally gone to ground in the agri-center.

The scratches? Received when wrestling through a wire fence, two—or was it four?—streets back.

"And can you identify these thieves?" the uniformed officer inquired.

"Of course," Ellison said, accepting a mug of tea from the keeper named Bren, while DS Hama and the two older keepers looked on. "Well, two of 'em, any road. One's a kid. One o' them dodgers as works the streets of a night. You know the type," he added, glancing Hama's way.

"And the other?" Officer Prudawe prompted, her tongue poking from between her teeth as she transcribed his statement into a spanking new notebook, oblivious of the mug Bren set at her side.

"Tall feller, and skinny with it," Ellison replied promptly. "Hair's sorta brownish-gray, not much to look at. Wears an infantry coat, and he's got himself a pet draco."

At which point the last mug, which Bren had been about to hand to DS Hama, tipped wildly, sloshing its contents over the floor.

Ellison watched as Hama looked at his tea, spreading across the tile, then up at the flushing youth.

"Something you'd care to share?" the detective asked Bren.

"It's just," Bren said as Thalia fetched a cloth, "that sounds a lot like one of our guests."

"Does this guest have a name?" Hama asked.

"It was Quinn," Bren said, Adam's apple bobbing. "Msr Gideon Quinn."

Meanwhile, in the house on Chaucer Street, Jessup Rand woke with a start, momentarily uncertain of his surroundings.

But with wakefulness came the realization he was in his study, where he'd joined Celia after seeing the last of their guests depart.

He and Celia had shared a drink, he recalled, and she had entertained him with her stinging observations of the various and sundry ristos who'd been their guests, but Jessup must have been much more tired than he thought, for he'd fallen asleep.

Tired, his querying mind prodded, *or old?*

Too old for the vibrant woman he'd married—*the woman he'd killed for*—and she'd left him there, snoring in his favorite chair.

Alone.

Unbidden, his fingers stroked over the chair's leather arm, taking comfort in its battered familiarity, as this particular chair had been through many a change with Jessup, following him from post to post, all the way back to the Academy. In fact, he'd often boasted he could trace his career in the various dings, stains, and scuffs that marked the oak-tanned aurochs-hide, from the wine stain of graduation day to the nick from a Midasian's sword in Upper Allianza.

That was the same post where Celia had missed the evacuating airship, he recalled, and thus been stranded, leading to Gideon Quinn's Twelfth Company being sent in to extract her.

This had led to Gideon Quinn setting eyes on Celia, and that had, in its turn, led to a cycle of violence and treachery that Jessup had struggled nearly seven years to forget.

On the arm of the chair, Jessup's hand clenched in a fist.

"Darling?"

He looked up to see Celia had entered the room, her gown whispering as she neared. Jessup, blinking, thought the red silk spilling from that single twist on her shoulder appeared more like a bleeding wound than the numbingly expensive dress it was.

"I fell asleep," he said, struggling to shed his exhaustion.

"I know." She stopped beside his chair. "I didn't have the heart to wake you, but then I got lonely." She held out a hand, and he, smitten as ever, took it, rising sluggishly from his chair to follow her out of the study.

At the base of the stairs, he paused. He'd been worried about something, had he not?

Quinn, he recalled. He'd been thinking of Gideon Quinn— the more so after hearing Killian's report. "Should have dealt with him the first time," he murmured.

"Dealt with whom?"

"What?" He shook his head and forced himself to focus on his wife, who was waiting. "Nothing. Just an old annoyance. It can wait."

"Good," she said, starting up the stairs again, "because I will be wanting all of your attention."

Jessup followed, thoughts of Gideon Quinn quieting to a dull echo.

All he knew, as she opened the door to the bedroom, was her smile, the soft sigh of her dress, her fingers in his hand, tightening in anticipation.

And then he was inside the bedroom, and there, sprawled at his feet in the flickering light of the fireplace, was Gideon Quinn himself, lying unconscious on the floor of the bedchamber.

He looked up. "Celia?" Her name was a question.

"Yes, I know, but as much as you deserve an explanation, I'm afraid we've run out of time."

"Celia, what are you talking about? Why is *he* here?" Jessup asked.

Or rather, meant to ask.

In fact, he only got as far as "Celia—" before Nahmin, who'd been waiting in the shadows, stepped up and slid something bright and cold between Jessup's ribs, piercing his heart so the rest of his questions went forever unvoiced, and so unanswered.

As he fell, however, Jessup did have time to wonder why Nahmin, bloodied blade in hand, was offering Celia a salute—and not the standard Colonial Corps salute, either, but the odd tap of the forehead that the Coalition forces favored.

Then he was on the floor, staring at the hated Gideon Quinn, which made him wonder . . .

CHAPTER 20

Gideon groaned his way to his third uncomfortable awakening of the night and, despite an unpleasant stickiness on the floor, counted himself lucky to be waking at all.

Not yet ready to face what was on the other side of his eyelids, Gideon took a slow, deep breath that caught midway at the familiar metallic scent thickening the air.

Damn, he thought, then forced his eyes open and yes, the scent was that of blood—a great deal of it—splattered on his shirt and slickly coating his now-unbound right hand where it lay directly in front of his eyes.

His right hand, and the knife he held in it.

Knife.

Bloody.

In his *hand.*

Gideon made himself look beyond the gory artifact to what he presumed was the source of all that blood and was on his feet before he knew he'd moved.

Then he stood, stunned and shaking, over the recently deceased Jessup Rand.

He looked at the body, then the knife he still held, then the body again.

"Huh," he said.

This seemed lacking, given the circumstances, but damned if he could think of anything else to say.

"How?" he then asked, which, while not much better, at least was a question.

It then occurred to Gideon he was having a very difficult time thinking past the thick, cottony fog. A fog, he realized, a lot like earlier that night when he'd been drugged by Nahmin, who worked for—

"Celia," the name ground out between his teeth as he at last remembered the woman in red pouring red liqueur down his throat, dosing him with morph.

Again.

There, see, his thoughts sloughed through the cotton; *you didn't kill Rand.*

I was drugged, so how do you know what I did and didn't do? He asked back.

"Because, you moron, you're left-handed," he heard himself say aloud, holding up his right hand, where he still held the knife.

He looked down at Jessup and felt the blade slide from his fingers to land on the floor with a *thud* that was almost as unpleasant as the sound of one man breathing when there were two men in the room.

More unpleasant still was the pounding of hurried footsteps rising from the street below, followed by the crack of a door being thrown open and the choked, fearful, yet viscerally recognizable voice of Celia Rand, begging those at the door to, "Please, hurry! They're upstairs . . . my husband and . . . and . . . the man who . . . he . . . he tried to . . ."

"Do not worry, Msr," an official-sounding voice interrupted Celia's dramatics, "we're here now."

She was a good liar; Gideon had to give her that.

She was also, he was certain, framing him for the murder of her husband.

He turned from the damning body of evidence in front of him to see that the rest of the room, which had been in pristine condition earlier, now looked as if a storm had swept through the picture window currently swinging open on its hinges.

A storm . . . or two grown men fighting over a woman.

She really did know how to set a stage, Gideon thought as the boots from outside hit the stairs.

Then he thought—*window*.

Thirty seconds later, the doors burst open and two of Nike's finest came rushing into the room, where they pulled up short in front of the body.

"Jessup!" Celia cried out before sliding to the floor in an apparent dead faint, which might also have led to a slight concussion as the two officers were paying no attention to her, being preoccupied by the presence of the body and absence of any apparent killer.

One of them was so new to the job that, while Celia was falling elegantly to the floor, young Officer Prudawe was racing to the open windows in hopes the fresh air would prevent any additional mess in the room.

Pressed against the building above the window, Gideon saw the dark head of a copper pop out.

He watched her shudder and heard the preemptive sound of retching.

While he sympathized, all he could think as she clutched at the sill was, *Don't look up. Don't look up. Don't look up.*

Then he made himself stop thinking that for fear the young officer would hear him thinking, and then she *would* look up and see the blood-spattered man balanced on the window's cornice, directly above where she was visibly trying not to puke.

His gaze remained locked on the officer's deep green cap as she placed her hands on the window ledge, one on either side of a bloody handprint.

Don't—the thought flitted out, in spite of himself.

She took several deep breaths.

—look—

Her hand slid a bit, and she raised it, turning the palm upwards to see the red smear.

—up.

She looked up.

"It's not what it looks like," he told her.

"Got him!" she shouted, disappearing into the room but reappearing a half second later, shooter in hand.

"That could have gone better," Gideon said.

"Sir," she said, "please climb down to be placed in custody."

Gideon considered the request. "I don't see how that can work out well for me."

On the street below, a compost lorry was chugging its way up the street.

"I'm telling you, you are under arrest!" the young officer called up, wildly brandishing the weapon.

"Have you been trained to use that thing?" Gideon asked, eyeing the lorry's progress.

Are you an idiot? his rational mind asked.

Now *you're paying attention?* Gideon asked the rational mind. *Where were you when Celia was drugging me?*

His rational mind had nothing to say to that.

"Yeah, I thought so," Gideon said aloud.

"What?"

"Sorry," he called down to the officer, "talking to myself."

"My mum says talking to yourself is a sign of mental instability," she told him. "Really, it'd be best if you climb back down here and let me arrest you."

Another head appeared in the window, and damned if it wasn't Mia's DS Hama, the decent cop, last seen on Marlboro Avenue.

"Hello!" Hama greeted.

"Hi," Gideon said with somewhat less enthusiasm.

By now the lorry had stopped directly below the cornice upon which Gideon was currently perched, this despite a lack of any bins needing emptying.

"Right mess in here," Hama called up to Gideon.

"Watch yourself, sir," the young officer said, pulling back as a draco swooped down past the window to buzz the lorry's cab.

"Yeah, about that," Gideon said, "you're going to have a hard time believing this . . ." he leaned out ever so slightly, " . . . but I was framed."

"Of course you were." Hama nodded his understanding. "Why don't you climb back in, and we can talk about it?"

"Or," Gideon said, "I could do this."

And he jumped.

Sadly, so did the young officer's trigger finger, which Gideon only knew because as he dropped, he experienced the too familiar burn of a plasma bolt.

Detective Sergeant Ishan Hama leaned out the window, tracking the lorry into which Gideon had successfully landed. "That's not something you see every day," he noted.

"But he's getting away," Prudawe said. "Shouldn't we pursue?"

"I don't imagine he will be going very far, at least not without the help of a physician," Hama said, glancing down at her sidearm.

She followed his gaze and, as he watched, her jaw dropped and her cheeks darkened. The shot counter listed one plasma bolt fired, just seconds ago.

"Oh, no," she groaned, powering down the weapon.

"It looked like a glancing blow, at worst," Hama told her. "That won't help with the paperwork, mind, but at least you didn't kill the man."

Both she and Hama leaned out the window.

"Best radio it in," he said, "and get an all-district alert on this fellow."

As Prudawe moved to obey, Hama pulled back into the bloody room to see a very unvalet-like valet caring for the vapor-ridden mistress of the house.

Hama hoped she recovered quickly—he had a few questions for the widow, not least of which was why she was wearing an infantry long-coat of a size more appropriate to a very tall man.

A man, he calculated, about the size of the fellow who'd just jumped two stories into a compost lorry.

CHAPTER 21

With one hand pressed to the plasma wound over his ribs, Gideon clung to the side of the compost lorry with the other and tried not to inhale the varying degrees of rot infusing the surrounding air. He had no idea how far they'd traveled but was getting woozy from the fumes.

"Do you even know how to drive this thing?" he yelled forward at the same time the vehicle came to a jerking halt

The lorry's engine hissed as the power was shut off, then the right-hand door popped open and a widely grinning Mia pulled herself up to peer into the lorry's bed. "Did you say something?" she asked, then narrowed her eyes as she got a good look at Gideon. "You could use another bath," she noted, her nose wrinkling.

"I asked if you could drive—never mind." He shook his head and started to climb out, only to be knocked back into the rubbish by a giddily swooping Elvis, who'd trailed the vehicle the entire way. "Ouch," Gideon said, then rubbed cheeks with the draco, who'd come to rest atop a mound of rotting greens to hiss his concern at his person.

"He was worried," Mia said.

"So was I." Gideon offered the draco one more gentle stroke before gritting his teeth and hauling himself out of the muck. "So should you be," he added, dropping next to her and tapping his right shoulder, where Elvis immediately came to rest, talons lightly pricking through the fabric of Gideon's shirt. "The cops won't be long tracking down a stolen compost lorry."

"I know. That's why I drove it here," she said, jerking her chin to the right.

Gideon followed her prompt, but in the monochrome of Nike's misty dawn, he could barely make out what he was seeing.

What first came to mind were the blocks his sergeant's daughter used to play with. She'd build these monstrous structures and then knock them over, laughing like a hyena as they went tumbling.

The buildings in front of him reminded him very much of those blocks . . . after the fall.

"Where is here?" he asked, following her as she headed into what had to be a condemned neighborhood.

"Lower Cadbury, or what's left of it, after the forty-seven bombings. Best get moving," she prompted as he seemed hesitant. "It's safe enough, and the coppers won't go in past the first two blocks."

"Because they don't have a death wish."

"The suns are never bright enough for you," she groused.

At that, Gideon had to laugh, then he hissed.

"Oy!" She poked at his side, apparently only just noticing what was going on under all the decayed vegetables. "You're hurt!"

"Ow," he said pointedly, and she dropped the poking finger. "One of the officers had a jumpy trigger finger."

"The coppers put that beating on you, as well?"

"No. Look, it's not so bad if I can get clean."

"Not sure there's enough water in the Avon for that," Mia said doubtfully but started to lead the way.

Gideon took one step after her, then froze as he realized something was missing. "She took it!"

"What?" Mia, already several steps ahead, looked back.

"That murdering wasp took my coat!" And as he said it, the loss hit him like a ton of Lower Cadbury's bricks.

"What wasp?" Mia started back. "Gideon?"

On his shoulder, Elvis began to croon anxiously.

In the distance, he could hear the wail of the police sirens.

And still Gideon didn't move—couldn't—as a kind of fugue settled over him.

"What's wrong with you?"

Unable to respond, Gideon shook his head, and that action caused the world to tip so drastically he had to lean forward and rest his hands on his knees.

"Gideon," Mia said, creeping up to touch his arm. "We gotta scarp."

He looked up, met her anxious eyes. "*You've* got to scarp," he said, forcing himself to stand up straight. "I'm done."

She blinked, then stared. "*What?*"

"I said, I'm done. Listen," he held up his bloodied right hand, the left still pressed to the seeping wound in his side, "it was bad enough when it was just Rand after me, except it wasn't Rand, or not *only* Rand because Celia was always there, playing me. Playing him too, I guess," he rambled, barely aware of Mia watching him the way one would watch a dog with the first hints of foam at its mouth. "The black swan who betrayed them all."

"Swan?"

"Played the cops, just now," he said. "Played them so well they're looking at me for Rand's murder."

She stayed where she was, watching. "Did you do it?"

"No. But I can't prove that." Any more than he could prove his innocence at Nasa. Rand—no, Celia—no, *Odile*—was just that good.

"I don't care what the filth thinks." Mia gave a shadow of her usual shrug. "I'm not sure I even care if you did for the bugger, I just care you're honest with me." She started to turn again.

"Mia." She stopped but didn't look back as he continued. "I'm not kidding. I'm done." She remained still, shoulders slumping in the tunic, which he now saw had a new tear in it. "You should get going," he said, but it was like talking to a wall—or himself, age thirteen. "Dammit, Mia—"

"*What?*" She spun around to face him, her hands flying out in exasperation. "*What?* What d'you want from me? A pat on the back? A handkerchief? What?"

"I—"

"So this wasp of yours . . ." She cut him off with a two-handed wave. "She put them mangy twins after you and had Nahmin dope you *and* set you up for a killin'?"

Gideon, watching the dodger the way he'd watch a grenade with a popped tab, nodded.

"She did all that, and now you're all 'boo-swarmin'-hoo, she has my coat'—"

"I don't believe I used those exact—"

"So you're *done*?" The hands, which had been continuing to flap in exasperation, dropped to her sides. "That's not done. That's quitting!"

"Well—"

"But all right. Fine. Quit. *Be* done." She shoved her hands in her pockets and glared with enough disdain he almost couldn't see the disappointment. "Done and dusted, and rotting inna nick because if you can't be bothered to get your own coat back from some fancy-pants upper-comber risto wasp—"

"Did I mention she's a fancy-pants upper-comber risto wasp spy?"

"Fancy-pants upper-comber risto wasp *spy*," Mia amended, "then what good are you?" Then she paused.

Gideon waited.

She looked at him. "Did you say *spy?*"

He opened his mouth to answer but didn't get a chance because just then, from somewhere nearby, they both heard a cry for help.

A cry that was suddenly truncated as if the one calling had been violently silenced.

"That way," Gideon said, gritting his teeth and launching himself past Mia. Elvis was already airborne, flapping his way deeper into the bombed-out tenements.

"We're not done with this," Mia called, but Gideon, with his long legs, was outpacing her, adrenaline doing its bit to make him forget his recent trials.

Mia, her own teeth gritted to the point of aching, raced after Gideon, catching up just in time to see him flying at a large, mean-looking tough. He tackled the bastard so hard they both went rolling over a pile of street rubble, so all Mia could see of the fight was the occasional fist or elbow.

The entire scene was punctuated by the odd grunt, curse, or screech—that last courtesy of Elvis—who was circling wildly above the fight.

Figuring Gideon had things under control, she turned to a young man who, from his prone position and ashen face, was the one who'd called for help, and offered him a hand up. "You okay there, mate?"

"I . . . Yes. I think." The youth patted himself absently as if making sure all his parts were still there. "I hope he doesn't hurt Wendell. That would only make it worse."

Mia looked at his bloodied lip, torn shirt, and scraped shoulder. "It could get worse?"

From behind the pile of rubble, a rough tenor shriek was followed by a significant *thump*, then Gideon's head popped up from behind the wreckage. "Everyone all right here?"

"I think it just did," the young man concluded.

"Wendell was after his monthly payment," the young man, who had introduced himself as Tiago, explained some forty minutes later.

He'd brought Gideon and Mia to his place in one of Lower Cadbury's remaining habitable buildings. Now Mia was parked at his kitchen table while Tiago made tea and Gideon stood in the door, buttoning the clean shirt Tiago had loaned him—after cleaning and dressing his wounds.

Lucky break, Gideon thought, coming to the rescue of a medical student. "I'm guessing this payment has nothing to do with rent," he said, beginning to roll up the sleeves.

"Security." Tiago confirmed the supposition while pouring hot water into the waiting teapot.

"A security racket? *Here?*" Gideon asked, looking at Mia.

"There's more a' that in Lower Cadbury than the other neighborhoods," she told him. "People with less to lose being more eager to keep what little they got."

"From the mouths of babes," Tiago murmured, laying a squashed packet of biscuits before Mia, which, Gideon had no doubt, was why Mia let that "babes" statement pass. "But, yes, Wendell's been running his protection scheme since about a year after the Adians dropped a payload on Lower Cadbury. And I pay him because if I don't, he'll burn my clinic down."

"I thought you was still a student?" Mia asked, crumbs spewing forth with the question, much to Elvis's delight. "Sorry."

"Fourth year," Tiago replied with a small smile. "But I was born in this neighborhood, so rather than pay more rent to live elsewhere, I live here for nothing and use my stipend for medical supplies for those in need."

"Damn," Gideon said.

"*Oy!* Language," Mia chided.

Gideon gave her a look, then sat down at the little table. "Tell me more about Wendell," he said to Tiago.

It was a story as old as Fortune.

Older, Gideon figured, as every bit of Earth's history he'd learned supported the notion that crime was as endemic to the human race as war.

In Wendell's case, it was a simple matter of being the toughest bully in Lower Cadbury, which had fallen on hard times when the enemy forces made their first and only successful attack on Avon's capital city.

Theory had it they were trying for the Corps Tactical Division to the city's north, but for reasons no one would ever know, had dropped their payload on the unsuspecting residents of the Lower Cadbury neighborhood.

Some of the survivors moved out, but there were many in Lower Cadbury too poor or too stubborn to relocate.

These were the people Wendell, with his crew of enforcers, promised to protect from burglaries, arson, and various other acts of violence.

Those who paid remained mostly untouched.

Those who didn't, or who were late on their payments, found themselves experiencing the aforementioned burglaries, arson, and acts of violence.

"So you can see how it might not look good for me," Tiago said as they all sat, sipping their tea, "you bashing the comb out of Wendell just now."

"And if he hadn't?" Mia, a study in indignation and biscuit crumbs, asked. "Wendell would'a bashed you proper, for sure."

"Physician, heal thyself," Tiago replied.

"Which might work, assuming Wendell didn't go for your hands," Gideon told him, causing Tiago's hands to twitch as he freshened Gideon's cup. "But I get your point. Wendell isn't going to go away." He looked at the young man. "Can you? Go away?"

"And leave my clinic? My patients?" Tiago shook his head. "I've got two elders with chronic cardiopulmonary distress, and a child about Mia's age with asthma. And every day brings a new trauma patient."

Probably, Gideon thought, because most every day someone's flat collapsed.

Or they forgot to pay Wendell.

"And what if someone could make Wendell go away?" Gideon heard himself ask.

"I . . ." Tiago seemed momentarily flummoxed. "I can't condone murder, if that's what you are asking."

"Oh, Gideon didn't kill no one," Mia assured the young man.

"Anyone," Gideon muttered.

"Gideon didn't kill *anyone*," she said, "but you can see how he facilitated the comb outta Wendell. And he did the same with the Ohmdahl triplets last night *and* some wanker named

Ronan and his sis. Gideon's Alpha Grade crystal when it comes to facilitating."

Both men found themselves staring at the chipper young dodger.

"What she means is, what if Wendell were to be . . . facilitated . . . out of the neighborhood?"

"Well," Tiago said, clearing his throat, "as long as there's no killing."

Which, of course, was when the first sirens started to sound.

"Police?" Tiago rose from the table. "They never come out here."

"Funny, that's what she said." Gideon glared at Mia.

She was already climbing out of her chair. "Maybe they take murder more serious than liftin' wallets?"

"Probably," Gideon agreed as he also rose, reaching automatically for his coat, which would normally have been draped over the chair.

"Wait," Tiago said, "you said you hadn't killed anyone."

"He didn't," Mia promised.

"It's complicated," Gideon added.

The sound of vehicles coming to a halt had them all freezing.

Sure enough, the next thing they heard were boots on the street, followed by some fairly vigorous thudding.

"They're knocking on doors," Gideon observed.

"They won't get a lot of answers," Tiago said. "Not too many live here, and those who do have little use for coppers who won't even walk a beat in this neighborhood."

"Time to scarp?" Mia asked.

Gideon looked at Tiago.

"If you head down to the basement, there's a gate to some old garden tunnels that are stable. I often use them during winter to get around."

Gideon looked at Mia, who nodded. "I've used 'em."

"You'll need this, though," Tiago said, turning to pull a hand torch out of a drawer.

"Thanks," Gideon said.

"One more thing." Tiago dashed from the kitchen, returning bare seconds later with his medical bag in hand. "You'll want these." As he spoke, he offered Gideon a stack of pain patches. "I'd give you something stronger but—"

"But I need to stay sharp." Gideon accepted the patches. "Thanks."

Mia slapped Tiago on the arm, which Gideon assumed was her version of a thank you, then dashed for the front door of the flat.

Gideon clicked for Elvis and followed as soon as the draco was settled. He could hear Mia's feet racing lightly down the stairs, but he paused and looked at Tiago, still standing in the kitchen archway, "Assuming I don't get sent up for a crime I didn't commit in the next few hours, I promise I'll do what I can to—facilitate—your situation. Until then, be smart and let these cops get you out of Cadbury. Tell them you saw me. They'll want you to come in and swear out a statement." He held up a hand as Tiago began to protest. "Your patients need you. I get that, but how much can you help them if you end up crippled . . . or a corpse?" He waited just long enough to see his argument take effect, then dove through the door, down the steps, and into the basement, hot on Mia's heels.

CHAPTER 22

Gideon was pleased to find that Tiago had been correct; the tunnels were stable.

Even better, the cops didn't seem to know they existed.

All of which was good.

Less good was the fact that the light shafts, which had once illuminated the tunnels, had long since collapsed, so their vision was limited to the narrow beam Tiago's torch provided.

"You're counting again," Mia said.

"Sorry." Gideon stopped.

"What are you counting anyway?"

"Steps."

She angled to stare up at him, half her face illuminated by the torch. "Why?"

"Long story," he said.

She looked as if she wanted to ask about the long story, but Gideon started moving again, leaving her little choice but to follow.

Eventually (after another 223 steps) Mia came to a stop.

"Here we are," she said, pushing through a half-open door.

"And here is?" Gideon asked, following into a basement that looked pretty much like Tiago's, except here there was a sliver of window letting in just enough light to see a floor covered in dust, rodent droppings, and gnawed-up bits of paper and wood.

"Part of a school," she explained. "Ain't been used since the blitz."

Something in her voice had him looking more closely at her. "How do you know about it?"

She looked at him. "Long story."

Had that coming, he thought, then strode over to peer out the window. "How safe is this place?"

"Safe as houses," Mia said, finding a relatively clean spot on the floor to hunker down.

Gideon turned from the empty street to look at her. "Have you seen the houses around here?"

"Double, double ain't no trouble gonna find us here, safe," she clarified.

That would have to do. "In that case," he said, crouching in front of where she'd folded herself into a small, hunched knot, "it's time to come up with a plan."

"For Wendell?"

"For everyone." He looked down at his hands, bruised and scraped and marked as a traitor, then up to see her watching him, her dark eyes uncertain in the dim light. "Starting with Celia Rand."

"The one who's a spy?"

"The one who's a spy. And then, of course, there's Killian Del, and the Fagin Ellison issue is still pending."

There was a silence as she stared, then looked down at her own grubby hands. "I thought you said you was done."

"*Were* done, and I thought I was." Had thought so, for too many years. "Guess I was wrong."

Of course, it wouldn't be simple.

Gideon's intention—to net Celia, Del, Wendell, *and* Ellison —would each require several elements.

"First, we need an irresistible lure; second, no possibility of collateral damage; and third—more than just you, me, and Elvis to execute properly," Gideon explained.

"I thought there weren't to be no killing," Mia said, her face splitting in a yawn.

"*Wasn't*, and *any*," Gideon corrected before he caught the yawn contagion himself. "In this case, execute means . . . facilitate. We need a team if we're going to facilitate the plan," he clarified, then fought off another yawn. "And maybe a nap."

"You go ahead. I'm fine."

Gideon looked at Mia, whose eyes were at half-mast. "Uh-huh."

"Well, I am. And anyway, don't you want someone t'keep watch?"

"Elvis will let us know if anyone gets too close. He has ears like a draco."

She groaned.

"Yes, the joke is lame," Gideon admitted, "but he does. Come on." He patted the floor as if it were a nice comfy mattress. "It's been a long night for both of us, and you didn't even get a morph nap like I did."

"Fine," she said, huddling up against the wall, "but don't blame me if the bad guys come upon us all unawares and like that."

"I promise, if any bad guys come upon us unawares and like that, I'll take full responsibility." He leaned against the wall and stretched his legs out in front of him, crossing at the ankle while Mia curled up next to him, grumbling only a little.

Elvis, who'd been roosting on the spindle of a broken chair propped in a corner, hopped over and stretched himself out on Gideon's leg.

Gideon let his head fall back against the chill wall while Mia's breathing slowed and Elvis's tail ceased to twitch.

It was almost homey, he thought.

Except for the creeping damp.

And the fact that he was being hunted.

And that Celia had his coat.

Gideon felt a shiver at his side and, without thinking, draped an arm over the sleeping dodger and was surprised when she burrowed deeper under his shoulder.

It was the sort of thing he thought a daughter might do, if he and Dani had ever . . . but sleep claimed him before he could finish the thought.

"How long will you be away, do you think?" Dani asked, leaning her chin on her crossed arms, her hair spilling over the pillow like black rain.

"No more than a month," Gideon said. "Less if there are no Midasians involved. What about you?"

"One week out to the drop zone, we do what we do in a day."

"Cocky."

"Confident," she corrected. "Another two days for the 'ship to scour the region, and a week back for resupply."

"Which means you'll be out on another mission by the time I get back."

"Life in the Corps," she said, turning to her side, so they were eye to eye. "The war won't last forever."

Gideon wished he could borrow some of her determined opti-

mism, but he'd been up close and personal with the enemy for far longer.

Dani's home colony of Fuji lay too far west for the Coalition forces to easily reach, meaning she'd grown up far from the conflict. Her childhood, at least, had been unclouded by air strikes and occupations and reprisals . . .

"Hey," she tapped the pillow, "Fortune to Quinn."

"Sorry," he said, but he did push down thoughts of endless battles to focus on the woman currently sharing his bed. It was still difficult for him to believe she was here. "You were saying?"

"I was saying, when it's over, you could come home with me."

"Home," he repeated the word, which felt foreign on his tongue.

"You'll like Tendo," Dani continued. "All of Fuji is beautiful, but Tendo's tree line goes all the way to the ocean, and we have snow in the winter. Kids," she added meaningfully, "really love snow."

Home, *he thought, staring,* and kids.

Practically in the same breath.

"Why are you looking at me that way? And if it's because you don't want children—"

"What? No," he said. "I mean, yes. I mean . . ." he paused, because he wasn't sure what he meant.

"Gideon? You're staring."

"Because you're not real." The words fell out before he could stop them. "I keep looking at you because I can't believe you're real," he admitted in a rush and then backtracked. "What I mean is, you couldn't—shouldn't—be here. Not with me, I mean. Keepers!" He flung himself onto his back and pressed his arm over his eyes. "Never mind. Just shoot me now and put me out of your misery."

"No, I think I understand," she said, pulling his arm down. "I'm just too good to be true, is that it?"

"You're too good for me," he said, meaning it.

"True," she agreed, though she was smiling as she said it, "but I'm also human, and therefore as flawed as the next person."

"Well, you do have odd taste in music." He tried to match her tone and failed miserably.

"Gideon," she murmured his name softly, then propped herself up on one elbow so she could trace her fingers along the line of his jaw, slowly and carefully, as if she were an artist and he her canvas. "Do you really need a reason for my being here?"

"No," he said, then sighed. "Maybe?"

She smiled. "Then let's just say that nature abhors a vacuum."

Ah, well, yes, that explained everything. Not. "So, what, I sucked you in?" he asked, though as her hand continued to explore, he started to lose the thread of the conversation.

Her smile went a little sad. "You have a big, empty space, in here," she told him, tapping his heart. Then she leaned closer, her warm lips brushing his neck, then his cheek, until they reached his ear where she could whisper, "Makes me want to fill up all the lonely."

"Hallooo, Fortune to Gideon!"

"Dani?" Gideon shot up from his crooked slump, dislodging Elvis and causing an unfortunate twang in his neck.

"Who's Dani?" Mia asked.

Gideon let out a pained breath. "No one," he said, hating that his voice sounded hollow—as it would if he had a big, empty space inside.

A Dani-shaped space.

Mia just looked at him, one hand soothing Elvis.

"Someone," he admitted. "Just . . . someone."

Mia looked at Elvis, who looked at her. The two seemed to have formed a bond. It was a comfort to Gideon, as it meant they'd be able to look after each other if the plan went swarm.

"Okay." He scrubbed his face the rest of the way awake. "Where were we?"

Mia's head tilted. "You was saying we needed an irresistible setup, no possibility of collateral damage, and a team."

"Were say—never mind." He shook his head, crossed his legs, and leaned forward on his knees. "First order of business, the team."

"This Dani gonna be part of it?"

"No," he said after a short beat, "but I think I know who will."

Then he told her.

Then he waited for her to stop laughing. "It's not that crazy," he said.

"The only thing more crazy is you thinking it's not that crazy."

"Maybe it's a little crazy, but it's an important part of the plan."

"I think I changed my mind," she said, sitting back on her heels. "You're better off quitting. Take your draco and run for it."

"Ha," he said.

"I'm serious," she said back.

"Okay." He straightened, mostly because he'd been hunched over so long. The light seeping through the small window had thinned some, as the suns rose above the nearby rooftops. "What, in particular, worries you?"

"What doesn't?"

"Listen, even if the guy's not as decent as you supposed, he's going to be more interested in getting to me than giving you grief. It'll be honey in the comb."

"Promise?" she asked.

He looked at her. "If I promised, I'd be lying, and I won't lie to you."

"In that case," she said, "I'll do it."

CHAPTER 23

Detective Sergeant Ishan Hama was, as Mia had surmised, a decent cop.

He took no bribes, believed in justice for all classes, and did his best to keep the peace in a city that had been under the cloud of a war that had taken not only his home but his husband, Paolo, who had gone down with the UCAS *Tenochtitlan*.

Even now, years after the fact, Ishan could too easily recall the numbing cold he'd felt the day he returned to the precinct, fresh from tamping down a potential riot, to see a captain of the Air Corps in his dress blues waiting by his desk.

Ishan was recalling that moment right now, in fact.

Probably because the young man seated next to his desk was the very image of a young Paolo.

"You okay, Dad?" Tiago asked.

"I am quite . . . okay," he said, hoping his son couldn't see the old distress. He cleared his throat, tapped his pencil, and shoved his untouched tea a bit to the left. "So, you believe you have seen the man we are looking for?"

"Yes, like I told Officer Prudawe ten minutes ago and DS Couerliane when she knocked on my door at home."

"Home." The word came out more as a derisive snort.

"Don't start," Tiago said.

"Of course not." Ishan waved his hands in parental frustration. "After all, what business is it of mine if my only son chooses to dwell in a derelict building, putting his life in danger every day for the sake of—"

"For the sake of our neighbors," Tiago said. "The same people who used to join us for tea in the morning, and to celebrate First Landing Day, and who came to Pai's funeral—"

"Don't start," Ishan echoed his son's earlier directive. He glanced around at the nearby desks, where other detectives and officers were suddenly very busy with the paperwork they usually avoided like a plague. "This is not the time," he added.

"It never is." Tiago sighed, slumping back in his chair as if he were fourteen and not twenty-four.

The two men sat so for another moment before Ishan moved his chair slightly, the squeak of wood against wood reminding him of the purpose of this interview. "About the suspect. Can you give me the description?"

"I already—"

"Told Prudawe and Couerliane. I know, but every time you tell the story, you may include another detail, and so we paint the picture one telling at a time, yes?"

"I'm sorry. Yes," Tiago said, then he took a long slow breath and began.

Dutifully, Ishan recorded that the man Tiago had seen was tall and thin and looked a right mess.

Riding in a compost lorry after being shot whilst jumping from a second-story window could do that. Ishan looked up when his son paused. "Is there anything else?"

"Right, umm." Tiago closed his eyes. "His hair was sort of

undecided," he said at last. "Not quite brown, not quite blond, but with some silver at the temples. I think there was a tattoo here." He pointed to the back of his own right hand. "And his eyes were blue."

Which matched the man Ishan had seen at the Rand townhouse, along with the description from the Elysium Inn.

Then he thought of the body of General Rand and the distraught widow . . .

". . . but he didn't seem like a bad sort."

"I'm sorry?" Ishan said, realizing with a start he'd been doodling rather than listening to his son's statement.

Tiago's mouth quirked in a slight smile. "I was saying, the man I saw, he was a mess, but he didn't seem like a criminal. He seemed decent."

"Perhaps he is," Ishan said, taking a sip of tea that hadn't been hot for nearly an hour. "But decent sorts are seldom found on the windowsill of a murder scene."

"He could have been framed," a new voice cut in.

Both men turned to see a young girl dressed in a roughly made tunic.

Ishan's eyes narrowed as he recognized her as one of the dodgers the Nike police were forever chasing. Before he could ask what she wanted, his eyes fell upon the draco riding on her shoulder. The beast had done an admirable job of camouflaging itself in her coiled hair but was now peering out of the dark curls and tasting the air with quick licks of its forked tongue.

It took everything Ishan had to suppress the childish glee the creature's presence elicited.

Tiago, meanwhile, hopped out of his chair. "Mia," he said, staring down at the child. "What are you doing here?"

"Did you get it?" she asked, ignoring his question as her eyes darted from Tiago to Ishan. "About him bein' in the window, so's maybe he was framed. Window? Frame?"

Neither man said anything.

"Pfft." She waved a dismissive hand. "Why do I bother?"

A few short but significant blocks from Lower Cadbury, Gideon was settling into a chair in the flat Mia had directed him to, watching a short, slender woman with dark hair bustle from the kitchen.

"Here." Sonja Ohmdahl, mother to the Ohmdahl triplets, pressed a Stolichnayan-style cup with a tooled allusteel holder into Gideon's hands.

"Thanks." He sniffed the tea with gratitude as he sat on a sturdy chair in the Ohmdahl's front room. He warmed his hands against the clear glass and tried not to stare at the Ohmdahl matriarch.

Apparently, Sonja Ohmdahl was used to this sort of speculation. "They don't come out that big, you know," she said with a knowing smile. "Especially triplets."

"I'd hope not," Gideon said, looking to where Rolf, Ulf, and Freya all stood in various states of bedhead—a wall of sleepy blond muscle at their mother's back.

Good humor aside, Sonja was still standing in front of Gideon, obviously waiting for him to drink his tea.

He raised the cup and smelled an abundance of lemon, typical of Stolichnayan tea, and took a tentative sip.

Bitter, bright . . . tasted like tea.

Just like the soup had tasted like soup, and the liqueur had tasted like liqueur, he reminded himself.

Yeah, but these are the Ohmdahls, his self said back. *The Ohmdahls don't do subtle.*

He drank half the cup in one swallow. "It's very good," he told Sonja.

"Of course it is," she said. "There is nothing like Kopernik tea to cure what is ailing you. Even if what ails is too much vodka, yes?" This last she addressed over her shoulder to her offspring.

"Yes, Mama," Freya replied, hefting her own cup and slurping enthusiastically.

"But it is not too much vodka ailing you, I think." Sonja turned back to Gideon. "I think what ails you has more teeth?"

"Actually," he said, setting the cup aside and leaning forward in the comfortable chair, "that's what I wanted to talk to your children about." Sonja's head tilted curiously, and the triplets, as if attuned to their mother's mood, became very attentive. "I wondered," he said to the three of them, "if you'd be interested in a job."

"A job?" Ulf perked up.

"What kind of job?" Sonja asked, giving her son a quelling look.

"A potentially dangerous job," Gideon admitted. "One that's unlikely to pay anything, but if it goes well, will put some very bad people away for a long, long time."

"This sounds like a terrible job," Sonja said. She looked at her children and sighed. "And you had them at 'dangerous.'"

"When do we leave?" Freya asked, confirming her mother's suspicions.

Gideon smiled. "Two things first," he said. "One, do you have a city directory, and two, would you happen to know where I could get my hands on a two-way radio set?"

In an unprecedented instance of good luck, they not only had the directory but also the radios, a holdover from the triplets' days in the Stolichnayan infantry.

"The solar pack is pretty old," Freya said, putting the radios in a carryall for Gideon. "It may only work for a few minutes."

"If this plan works the way I hope, a few minutes is all I'll need," Gideon assured.

"That," Sonja observed, "is a very big 'if.'"

Mia wouldn't say DS Hama's reception was particularly honey-like, but at least he wasn't looking to clap irons on her.

And finding Tiago here had been a nice surprise.

"You know this girl?" Hama asked Tiago.

"I—it's complicated," Tiago offered weakly.

"Funny." Mia picked up the noticeable slack. "That's what Gideon always says."

"Gideon?" Hama looked at her.

"Does Gideon know you're here?" Tiago asked.

"*Gideon?*" The detective echoed himself, rising to stare at Tiago. "You *know* Gideon Quinn?"

"Not know so much as . . . we've met."

"When Gideon saved Tiago here from a thug what was asking protection money," Mia said brightly.

"*Not helping,*" Tiago murmured.

"Protection?" Hama turned on Tiago. "You said your lip was split by a fevered patient."

"Dad," he began.

"OY!" Mia jumped on that. "DS Hama's your *dad?*"

"It's—"

"Stop! Both of you! Be silent," Hama snapped.

Mia and Tiago shared a glance, but they remained silent, as did everyone else in the room.

"You," Hama pointed to Mia, "wait your turn. *You,*" he said, turning to Tiago, "why did you not say you'd *met* Quinn? You know he is dangerous."

"You're right about that. He is dangerous," Tiago said,

ignoring Mia's warning hiss. "But I don't believe he is a murderer."

Hama closed his eyes for a moment, and his lips moved.

Mia, staring at him, realized he was counting.

"Very well," he said upon reaching the number ten, "what makes you believe—despite having been found at the scene, covered in the blood of the man who put him in prison—that Quinn is not a murderer?"

"Because he's . . ." Tiago seemed to flounder a moment before landing. "Because he really is decent."

Mia smiled.

Hama stared at his son for a moment, his face devoid of expression, then he turned to Mia. "Your turn," he said. "Why did Quinn send you to the police?"

"He didn't send me to the police," she said, shaking her head. "He sent me to you."

"Me?" Though why that should surprise him more than any of the other revelations, he didn't know. "Why?"

"Because," she said, looking from Hama to Tiago and back, "you're decent."

Hama stared. Possibly counting again.

Then Hama sighed. "Perhaps you should tell me what your Msr Quinn wants."

***

Once in possession of the radios and addresses he needed from the directory, Gideon laid out the Ohmdahls' portion of the plan.

Once he had, and Sonja had promised to reinforce both the instructions and the timing, *repeatedly*, he took his leave, heading back to the Elysium Inn. He entered through the back door and strode into the kitchen as preparations for lunch were underway.

"Msr Quinn?"

He looked left, to where the young keeper who'd delivered his dinner was up to his elbows in potato peelings.

"Hi," he said brightly. "Keeper . . ."

"Bren," Bren filled in automatically, shaking peel from his hands. "And that's Keeper Thalia. Or it was," he added as the middle-aged keeper who'd been sautéing onions at the grill, had left the room.

Hopefully not to teleph the coppers, Gideon thought.

"Keeper Bren," he said, smiling. "I don't suppose my room is still available?"

"What? Oh! Yes. You're paid up through tomorrow, but—"

"Great, that's great. With any luck, I'll be needing it tonight."

"Only did you—"

"I also wondered if there's a Hive Master in the inn I could speak to?"

"There is, and he's here," a deep voice boomed across the kitchen.

Gideon turned to see a man of medium height, burly build, and a no-nonsense expression enter the kitchen at Thalia's side.

"I'm Master Donal," the man continued. "And you'd be Gideon Quinn, would you not?"

"Yes, sir."

Donal's eyes narrowed.

"I told you," Bren began, but when Donal shot him a look, closed his mouth so fast Gideon heard his teeth clack.

"Tell me," the Hive Master addressed Gideon, "what were you doing in my winter wheat last night?"

"I wasn't in your winter wheat last night," Gideon said. "I did mess with your composter, so I guess I owe you some damages to the wall," he added. "And then there was an issue with my bathroom window, for which . . . okay, I don't have any cash left, but maybe we could work something out?"

"Never mind that, for now." Donal waved it aside as Bren's face split into a grin.

"I told you," the youth said again. "That Ellison fellow was off the mark."

"Ellison was here?" Gideon asked, then shook his head before muttering, "It really is a comedy of errors."

"I love that play," Bren beamed.

"Bren . . ." Donal shot the youth a warning glance, then focused on Gideon. "Msr Ellison was hiding in the wheat field and accused you and a dodger of having attacked him."

"From what I've heard of him, that tracks," Gideon said. "He's a fagin," he explained to the waiting keepers. "And he abuses his dodgers—I've seen evidence of it," he added, his gaze going dark. "I mean to stop it."

"Interesting," Donal said, his own expression shifting. "You do know the police are looking for you?"

"And I intend to let them find me," Gideon said. "Eventually."

"Eventually?" Donal's brow arched in curiosity.

"Yes, sir," Gideon said. "But before then, I wanted to ask a favor. I've been out of the world a while, but I'm hoping keepers still offer sanctuary?"

"We do," Thalia said before Donal could respond.

"As my wife says," the Hive Master echoed. "Though if you're requesting sanctuary from the police—"

"No—well, yes—but not for me," Gideon said.

"All right," Donal said, arms crossing over his barrel of a chest. "Let's hear what it is you're wanting."

Erasmus Ellison was cooling his heels in the outer lobby of the Ninth Precinct, something he'd successfully avoided for years. But that Hama fellow had insisted Ellison needed to swear out a warrant against his alleged attacker, Gideon Quinn.

Now here it was, well into the day, and his dodgers would be back at the hive, unsupervised, where Ellison was sure they'd be helping themselves to a portion of the night's takings, leaving him just enough to avoid a beating.

Bad enough Mia was running loose with that thrice-damned draco, he'd not lose an entire night's take just to help the coppers search for this Gideon bleeding Quinn.

Disgusted, he rose from the narrow slice of bench he'd managed to hang on to, fully meaning to scarp, when he spied Mia in the company of half a dozen coppers, including Hama and Prudawe.

Oddly, Mia wasn't being hauled in by the filth, but rather leaving the building in their company, chatting easily with a civilian youth and, most damning of all, that bloody draco on her shoulder.

Ellison was shocked, not so much by her presence, but by the way she stood tall, her hands moving expressively, her face open and relaxed in a way he'd never seen.

It never once occurred to him that this was what happiness looked like.

What did occur to him, once he was able to see past the red haze, was that she was going somewhere *with* the coppers.

Not twenty seconds later, he was out the door, watching her climb on the back of DS Hama's mag-cycle, while the youth straddled Officer Prudawe's vehicle. All around them, officers were hopping on their rides, checking their weapons, all practically glowing with eager efficiency.

Ellison hated every bleeding one of them.

As cycles hummed to quiet life, he glanced around and, *oy!*

It looked as if some honest citizen had left their Edsel Comet right in front of the station, mistakenly assuming their property would be safe in front of the coppers' house.

What honest citizens never thought was how many criminals passed through the precinct on a daily basis.

Less than half an hour after meeting Gideon, Donal, Bren and two other keepers departed the Elysium, carrying one of the Ohmdahls' radios.

Gideon followed a few minutes later, in possession of the other radio, as well as the faintest hope that his plan might actually work.

If, that is, Mia had been able to persuade DS Hama to follow her lead, and *if* the Ohmdahls played their roles effectively, and *if* the targets responded as Gideon expected.

A lot of ifs, he told himself.

If you have any better ideas . . .

Not surprisingly, his self had nothing to offer.

CHAPTER 24

Unfortunately for Martin Soong, Clive had chosen to bring his mood, along with his fine collection of bruises, to Martin's pub, the aptly named A Fine Mess.

For the past hour, Clive had been muttering over his glass, complaining about the soldier who'd given him a beating, then segueing into muttering over his own crew, which was apparently made up of, ". . . a passel of morons what couldn't find their own arses in a blackout!" he exclaimed, loudly enough Martin almost dropped a bottle.

"One man," Clive continued to moan, leaning his forehead on the bar in front of him. "One sodding bugger, and not a one of my boys can find 'im."

"Hard luck, that," Martin commiserated, though not very enthusiastically, given he was one of the many in Lower Cadbury forced to pay Wendell for the privilege of not having his business burn to the ground.

"It'll go a lot harder on him," Wendell said, raising his head to stare expectantly at his empty glass.

Martin took the hint and dug out the good stuff, which was

only slightly less likely to eat a hole in one's stomach lining than the bad stuff, and poured. "Never seen the fellow before, then?"

"Didn't I say that?" Wendell tossed the liquor back and then coughed. "Bloody Earthers, man, why can't you serve somethin' less lethal?"

Because I can't afford it, Martin thought. *Because all my profits go to making sure you and your lot don't burn my joint and break my fingers.* "Inflation," he said with a shrug.

"Swarmin' economy'll bleed us all to death," Wendell griped, downing the rest of his drink.

Martin, wisely, said nothing and poured another shot.

"I'll tell you what, though," Wendell said as he eyed the glass greedily. "I'll be payin' a visit to yon Doc Hama, I will. It was 'im yapping that brought the tall bugger, so's maybe I get 'im yapping again, the tall bugger'll make another appearance. Only this time it'll be me and my boys waiting."

"And won't that be fun," Martin murmured.

"Whazzat?"

"Nothing," Martin said, tipping another slosh into the glass. "Only you *do* know Tiago Hama's father is a cop?"

Wendell was apparently unimpressed. At least the *pfffft*-like noise he made sounded unimpressed. "What good are coppers in Lower Cadbury?"

What good, indeed, Martin thought.

"Only law here," Wendell continued, on a roll, "is mine."

Maybe I could pack up shop and move, Martin thought. *I hear Edsel's nice this time of year.*

"What?" Wendell started to stand.

"What?" Martin asked, afraid he'd used his outside voice until he realized Wendell wasn't talking to him but to the man who'd just walked in. "Hello?"

"Good day to you, Msr Bartender," the man greeted Martin. "Rolf Ohmdahl, at your service. But excuse me; I have been some time looking for this piece of mammoth dropping here." As he spoke, his gaze shifted to Wendell.

Wendell's tiny eyes glittered with menace. "Are you talking to me?"

"Did I not say this?" Rolf beamed. "For you, Msr Wendell, I have a message from my good friend, Gideon Quinn."

"And who the flamin' turd is Gideon Quinn?"

Martin, with that uncanny instinct of bartenders from ancient Earth to modern Fortune, began removing Wendell's glass, the bottle, and any other incidental breakables, from the bar.

"Gideon Quinn is . . ." Here Rolf paused, his mighty forehead screwing up in thought. "Ah yes, Gideon Quinn says to say, he is the man who pounded your sorry ass into the pavement early this morning, and if you know what is good for you, you will be taking yourself and your bottom-feeding enforcers out of Lower Cadbury by sundown."

"Know what's good for *me*?" Wendell asked, visibly shocked.

Martin could understand this, as thus far no one had dared stand up to Wendell.

Well, that one gal had, an ex-corpsman, she'd been.

Her body had been found floating in the Avon the next day.

"So he says." Rolf nodded.

"And does this Gideon Quinn say what'll happen if I don't *know what's good for me*?"

"Wait, I must think," Rolf said, looking a bit troubled. "Ah!" He pointed a massive finger upwards as if remembering something. "Yes. He says if you are unwilling to take the easy way, you should be going to 919 Penelope Street, at sixteen hundred hours, that is being two in the afternoon, for you civilians," he added helpfully.

"I know what swarming sixteen hundred hours is," Wendell

snarled, but Martin knew he was lying because Wendell had never enlisted, preferring to hide out in the bombed-out ruins of Lower Cadbury and make war on the survivors.

"Then you will be prompt," Rolf said with a smile. "Or you will be gone, yes?"

"Yes," Wendell said. "Wait, I mean no! No, I will not be gone from Lower Cadbury. I'll bleedin' burn Lower Cadbury to the ground before I leaves it."

"Funny," Rolf said, though now he was absolutely not smiling, "that is what Quinn says you would say." He looked at Martin. "Goodbye, Msr Bartender."

"Bye?" Martin said, half-raising the soiled bar rag at the departing Rolf, not entirely certain what had happened here.

"Two o'clock," Wendell muttered, rising from the stool and heading for the door. "I'll be ready *before* two o'clock. Me *and* my bottom-feeding' enforcers will take 'im by surprise, and then we'll see what's good for me."

Martin watched Wendell stalk—well, limp, really—away, and decided it would be wise to close up shop for the day.

If not the week.

A flurry of motion had the desk sergeant of the Ninth Precinct looking up from a pile of briefs, then standing to full attention.

It wasn't every day a general walked in the front door. "Sir," she greeted the incoming brass. "How may I—"

"General Kimo Satsuke, Corps Special Operations. Where is Detective Sergeant Hama?" the general asked, overriding the greeting.

Sergeant Tyree blinked and noted a sympathetic grimace from the captain at the general's side. "DS Hama is in the field," she said to Satsuke. "Would you like me to take a mess—"

"Where did he go?"

"I believe he was following up on an active lead. I'm sure if you'll—"

"Was this lead regarding the murder of General Jessup Rand?"

"If I may ask, how did you know—"

"General Rand is—*was*—the commanding officer of the Tactical Division," Satsuke said. "As such, DS Hama forwarded his report to Tactical HQ, who forwarded it to CSO, who forwarded it to me, as my airship was already en route to Nike."

"But why—"

"General Rand's death is a matter of Colonial security, as is this investigation," Satsuke continued to answer the sergeant's half-asked questions. "So, did DS Hama's pressing lead have anything to do with General Rand?"

The sergeant decided this was above her pay grade. "He didn't mention, specifically."

Satsuke's eyes narrowed. "Did he mention anything nonspecific?"

"He said . . . he said he was following a wild draco."

The general grunted, then looked at the sympathetic captain.

"It sounds like him," the captain said with a tip of the head, her long black hair swinging with the motion.

The general turned back to the sergeant. "How do I find DS Hama?"

The sergeant turned and spied an officer at loose ends. "Arroyo! Please show General Satsuke to the radio room."

Officer Arroyo snapped to attention. "This way, General." He started for the double doors, which led into the precinct operations rooms.

Satsuke grimaced her thanks—at least, Tyree chose to

believe thanks were involved somewhere in the twist of a scowl
—and gestured for the captain at her side to follow.

"Your man," Satsuke told the captain as they passed through
the doors, "has mucked this up properly."

"He's not my—yes, sir," the captain agreed. "He does that.
But if he remains true to form, the muck will fertilize a solid
crop."

"You know I hate metaphors," Satsuke snapped.

As the doors swung closed, Tyree returned her attention to
the common burglary, brawls, and blackmail to which she was
accustomed, and which, thankfully, had nothing to do with colonial security.

Shortly after thirteen o'clock, Nahmin knocked on the door of
General Rand's office.

"Come in," Celia's muffled voice called, and Nahmin
entered to find the lady of the house rifling through the general's
plain metal desk.

"Sir," he said, "there was a teleph on the main house line
from the Ninth Precinct. They wanted to let you know Quinn is
still at large."

"Imagine my surprise." She brushed a lock of hair from her
cheek as she opened a file bearing the Eyes Only stamp.

"You have doubts about the efficiency of Nike's police
force?" he asked.

"On the contrary, I have no doubt whatsoever that they will
fail to apprehend him."

"That doesn't worry you?"

"Not particularly," she said, laying down the file. "Jessup,
whatever his faults, was meticulous about his work. There
isn't a shred of evidence indicating Jessup framed Gideon in

Nasa, while everything points to Gideon as Jessup's murderer."

Nahmin had to admit, it seemed quite rational when she said it.

But then, Celia's particular skill was her ability to make the unthinkable seem perfectly reasonable in the eyes of her assets.

It was said skill that had Colonial engineers placidly handing over mockups of the latest in weapons technology during an assignation, and airship captains sharing flight plans over a glass of wine.

"Still," he began, then paused as the doorbell rang. "Are we expecting anyone?" he asked.

Celia frowned. "No, but my sudden bereavement may have reached the ears of the gentry." She slid the files back into the drawer and locked it. "Best answer the door," she said, stacking the papers she'd culled. "We shouldn't disappoint the maudlin hordes."

Nahmin did as she asked, but when he reached the door, he opened it not to a curious neighbor but to Rey and Ronan Pradesh.

"We found Quinn," Rey said, elbowing her way past Nahmin.

"Not we," Ronan corrected.

"Then who has?" Celia asked from behind Nahmin. "Surely not the police."

"The Ohmdahls," Rey said, glaring at her brother.

"Do we know any Ohmdahls?" Celia asked Nahmin. "Are they on the social register?"

"Hardly," Nahmin replied. "The Ohmdahls are apparently friends of the twins. They helped us apprehend Quinn the first time."

"How lovely." Celia turned her attention to the twins. "And have they apprehended him for you again?"

"No," Ronan said. "But Freya Ohmdahl told us they spied him passing through their neighborhood, so she and Rolf followed him to some busted-up shack on the docks. She also said he looked bad. Injured, maybe, or sick."

"I suppose being shot while jumping from a window could do that," Celia murmured before asking, "How well do you know these Ohmdahls?"

"Pretty well," Ronan said.

"Well enough to know they're not the quickest drones in the hive," Rey added.

Celia hummed. "Is it possible they only saw what Gideon wanted them to see?"

"I'd give it fifty-fifty odds," Ronan said, after a considering beat.

"In that case," Celia mused, "it would be a pity to disappoint him."

"We can take care of him," Rey said, her eyes flashing.

"Then I will leave him in your most capable hands," Celia said. "Only this time, there is no need to leave him breathing."

"Understood," Rey said, sharing a quick grin with her brother.

Celia waited until the twins had departed to turn to Nahmin. "Best follow them, to make absolutely certain it's done."

"Sir," he nodded, offering a brief Midasian salute before making his own departure, determined that, one way or another, the troublesome Msr Quinn would soon cease to be a problem.

CHAPTER 25

THE CLOCKS WERE CHIMING FOURTEEN NOON WHEN ISHAN Hama, Mia, Tiago, Prudawe, and four other officers from the Ninth Precinct House stepped onto the sagging riverside dock.

Ishan, breathing through his teeth, found it amazing that, despite over a decade of disuse, the place still reeked of fish.

"Not much left of it, is there?" Officer Prudawe asked, eyeing the slumping excuse for a boathouse that sat midway along the finger of rotting wood Mia had led them to.

"Puts me in mind of an Ancient Earth abstractionist my husband was fond of," Ishan replied. "Any second now, and it will melt into the river."

At his side, Mia shrugged, upsetting the draco, Elvis. "It's not so bad as it looks," she said a bit defensively.

Ishan imagined she was right. He imagined it was a great deal worse than it looked. "Why would Quinn choose this place for a meeting?"

At the question, she shrugged again, but her eyes weren't on the boathouse; they were scanning the surrounding area, as if she were looking for something.

Or someone.

Quinn? Ishan wondered. He also looked around, but there was no one, and nothing, to be seen. Only the river, gray in the overcast winter light, and the length of dock, strewn with rotting bits of hemp and upended fishing boats with their hulls staved in.

And, of course, the boathouse, which was, at Mia's urging, their destination.

"He don't want to cause no trouble," Mia had explained, looking remarkably at ease in the Ninth Precinct's detective pool.

The girl was now seated in the chair Tiago had been occupying, while the draco perched on the chair's back and added the occasional chirp or hiss to the conversation, like a reptilian chorus of sorts.

"If last night is an example of Quinn not wanting to cause trouble," Ishan said, "I shudder to think what would happen if he did want to."

"I already told you, he didn't do no murder," the girl protested.

"But he did, at your own admission, do damage to private property, commit at least one theft, and instigated public mayhem."

"The damage weren't on him," she said, loyal to the last. "And it was more borrowing of private property."

Ishan smiled thinly. "And the mayhem?"

"Depends," she said, scritching the draco under its chin.

"On what?"

"On what mayhem means."

Tiago, standing over the young pair, smiled at that. "It means to cause a commotion," he told the girl. "Among other things."

"Oh," she said, biting her lip as she thought. "Yeah, I suppose he done that."

"My point," Ishan said, "is that whatever your Msr Quinn meant, his presence has caused all manner of trouble for the citizens of Nike."

"Except it ain't Gideon's bein' here that caused the troubles," Mia said, her eyes glimmering with determination. "The troubles was already there, hiding' like, until he come in and turned on the lights."

Ishan still wasn't certain he agreed with Mia's assessment of Quinn's presence in Nike, but he had agreed to accompany her here, to a section of the Avon docks that had been abandoned for many years.

The party was perhaps twenty paces from the boathouse when Ishan spied movement through an open sliver of wall.

He held up a fist, and the other officers drew their weapons.

He gestured in a circle, and they peeled off to surround the building.

"Stay here," he ordered Mia and his son.

Mia looked ready to protest, but Tiago put a gentle hand on her arm—not too close to the draco—and she settled back.

Ishan started for the boathouse door, his own weapon charged and ready in his hands.

Despite Mia and Tiago's assurances to the contrary, nothing he'd learned thus far of Quinn indicated he was anything *but* dangerous. Because of this, when the door he approached began to creak open, it took an act of vigorous will not to shoot first and apologize later.

He was particularly relieved he'd resisted the urge when a keeper, in full Hive Master colors, opened the door.

"DS Hama." Donal's face split into a grin. "We've been expecting you."

"That is very interesting," Ishan said, carefully easing his finger away from the trigger, "as I was in no way expecting you." Then he paused. "We?"

In answer, Donal swung the door further open, allowing Ishan to see who else was inside the boathouse.

"Sir?" Prudawe called, from his right.

"Weapons down!" he called out, then looked at Mia, who was trotting up to join him. "I don't suppose you would care to explain."

"It's complicated," she said.

"And best discussed inside," Donal added, opening the door and gesturing expansively within. "As I believe more company will be on the way shortly."

"And Quinn is not here, I take it?" Ishan asked the keeper as they entered, and Tiago immediately crossed the room to where the handful of children waited.

"Msr Quinn had other business to see to," Donal explained. "But he did ask me to deliver a message."

Ishan turned to Mia, who was digging through some rubbish at the far end of the boathouse.

"I never actually said he'd be here," she told him, not looking up from her labors.

He shook his head and looked at Donal. "And the message would be?"

"The message was to be delivered in three parts," Donal said, clearly enjoying his role. "The first being, 'You're welcome.'"

Ishan had never been a tooth grinder, but even now, he could feel his teeth beginning to grind. "For what?"

It was Mia who answered. "For this," she said, emerging from the rubbish pile with a lockbox, which she proceeded to drag across the floor. "I already unlocked it," she added, a bit breathless as she stopped next to the detective and the keeper.

Ishan looked at the box, then at the mass of children, then at Donal.

Holding his breath, he opened the box.

He let out the breath and stared down for a moment, then looked at Mia.

"That's just the small stuff," she said, rocking back on her heels as she also examined the contents. "Easy to stash, easy to fence, if need be."

"I could retire on this," Ishan said numbly.

"I could finally get the underground agri-center finished," Donal added with a huff.

"Gideon thinks we should give back as much as we can," Mia said with only a hint of disgust.

"*Gideon* thinks?" Ishan looked up.

"It was also his suggestion," Donal inserted, "that the children, having suffered under a cruel and corrupt influence, be offered sanctuary."

Ishan felt a bit weak in the knees. "And does this corrupt influence have a name?"

"Ellison," Mia said, the name falling from her tongue like acid. "Erasmus Ellison, our fagin."

On the other side of the room, a small child of undetermined gender cursed the sound of that name.

"And that would be the same Erasmus Ellison who claimed Gideon trounced him in your wheat field?" Ishan asked Master Donal.

"It was Elvis here who trounced Ellison," Mia said proudly.

Ishan looked to the rafters, where Elvis was observing the proceedings. "Good on Elvis," he murmured, wondering how on Fortune he'd write up this report. "Keeper sanctuary is your privilege, and the children's choice," he told Donal. "Though I will wish to take their testimony against the fagin."

"We'll give it, right?" Mia looked at the dodgers, small and solemn and hungry, who all nodded—some enthusiastically, some fearfully—but all most definitely.

"Bravely done," Ishan said to the children, then looked at Donal. "And what is the second part of the message?"

"The second part is more in the way of being a favor," Donal said.

"What sort of—" Ishan began, only to be interrupted by Elvis, swooping down to Mia's shoulder with a low keen.

"I believe," Donal said as Mia's eyes, wide and frightened, met his, "you're about to find out."

Ronan and his sister both had their shooters at the ready as they approached the decrepit boathouse where Freya claimed Quinn was hiding.

"Movement," Rey whispered, and both went still, their gray clothing blending into the warped wood of the dock.

Ronan peered up through the hood of his tunic to see the hint of a shadow passing the cracked glass of a window.

"Door or window?" he asked, his voice barely a whisper.

"Door," she mouthed. "High and low."

He nodded and, as one, the siblings made a fast, hunched-back dash for the crookedly hung door, where Rey took hold of the knob, yanked it open, and ducked under Ronan's arm as both dove into the room, he high and right, she low and left.

"Eat plasma, Quinn!" he called recklessly, finger already tightening on the trigger.

Except there was no Quinn to take out.

Instead of the lean soldier, there stood a robust-looking

keeper, his teeth bared, along with a half-dozen coppers, weapons active and raised, spread throughout the room.

One of the coppers was standing against the wall to Ronan's right, close enough Ronan could feel the vibration from his pistol.

"You know how this works," the bearded man said, stepping forward. "Do the needful, or I will have you smoking on the floor before you can count to one."

As the two invaders, their eerily similar faces dark with fury, laid down their arms, Ishan heard Tiago's whispered cheer from the other side of the boathouse where he, the children, and the other keepers had been huddling behind the rubbish pile. This filial approbation was immediately followed by Mia's in no way whispered, "Your dad's a right badass!"

Ishan suppressed a smile and stepped back as Officers Prudawe and Stoltz put the two would-be killers in irons.

Any day he could impress the youth of Nike was a good day, he supposed, though he still had no idea who these twins were or why they should be wanting to kill Gideon Quinn.

And then Donal cleared his throat.

At least, Ishan assumed the noise that came out like a mason's power grinder was the Hive Master clearing his throat.

"Now it is time for the third part of the message," Donal said, handing over a Stoli infantry radio that had seen far better days. "Msr Quinn sends this, with his compliments, and asks you to turn it on as soon as you are within range of General Rand's residence but also asks that you not enter the house until he makes direct contact."

Mia, who'd already been impressed by DS Hama's cool apprehension of the twins, was even more enamored of the detective's varied and creative swearing. "I ain't even heard some of them words," she confessed to Tiago.

"I think he's inventing a few new ones, just for the occasion," Hama's son replied.

"Cor," Mia said, shaking her head in admiration.

Outside, a few dozen meters downstream from the boathouse dock, Nahmin watched the procession make its way to land.

The unusual parade consisted of a mix of law enforcement —civilian and keeper—as well as a number of children, a young man of no obvious profession, and a draco flying over the lot.

There were also Rey and Ronan Pradesh, both being led away in shackles.

Of Gideon Quinn, there was no sign.

Which meant Gideon Quinn was somewhere else.

Nahmin had a terrible feeling he knew *exactly* where that somewhere else was, so by the time the procession was heading toward a nearby warehouse, Nahmin was already racing for his own transport.

Just north of Nahmin's position, Erasmus Ellison hunkered in the wreckage of an old ferry left to ruin on the shore and watched the keepers, dodgers, and coppers—these last carrying his lockbox—walking away.

With a stealth that belied his bulk, the fagin trailed the lot, and when they reached their cycles, clustered in the ruins of an old Tenjin Corp warehouse, he listened to DS Hama dispatching his officers like a general ordering troops, some to deliver the man and woman they'd nicked to the precinct and others to attend him to some risto's house near the city's center.

Ellison waited for the coppers to ride off on their cycles, again with Mia riding pillion behind Hama and the draco flying off after them.

Then he waited until the keepers and the youth, with his dodgers in tow, made their way out of the ruins of the old dockyards.

Once the coast was clear, he made a beeline for the stolen Comet, which he then drove at a calm and considered pace to Chaucer Street, which was the location Hama had announced as his next destination.

CHAPTER 26

Killian Del heard of General Rand's death as soon as he woke, shortly before fourteen noon.

He learned of the tragedy not via the newspaper presented on his breakfast tray, but rather through the oldest and most effective information delivery service known to humanity . . . the servants.

In his case, it was his butler, who had it from the downstairs maid, who had it from the cook, who had it from the grocery driver, whose morning delivery to the Rand home had been turned away by the police officers investigating the general's murder.

Upon learning of his friend's demise, Killian chose to forego his usual second cup of tea and instead telephed the city's Chief of Police to demand a face-to-face meeting.

Killian didn't feel Chief Salla had shown sufficient deference, but she did agree to stop by as soon as was feasible.

The lack of urgency on the chief's part had Killian rethinking his endorsement of Salla come the next city election because, while it looked good to be seen backing a non-corrupt official, he'd never expected *non-corrupt* to also mean *noncompliant*.

Determined to rectify the issue, Killian used the time between their teleph conversation and Salla's arrival to review his personal ledgers with an eye toward which of the officials listed therein would prove a more agreeable successor.

He'd just narrowed down the possibilities to a District Commander already in his pocket and a second cousin who'd served as a captain in the Civil Defense Service, when Chief Salla was announced.

Killian set the books to one side as Salla was shown into the office, just as the university bells chimed half-one.

"Chief Salla," Killian greeted, neither rising nor offering the chief a seat. "I trust you had sufficient reason to keep me waiting."

"There was a bit of a crime spree throughout the Ninth District last night," Salla replied, seeming untroubled by Killian's lack of courtesy. "The sort of thing the chief of police is expected to attend to."

"And is this neighborhood not part of the ninth district?" Killian demanded. "Jessup Rand was *murdered*, not three blocks from here. Who was attending to the general? Where," he added, leaning back with his hands steepled beneath his chin, "was the police presence on Chaucer Street?"

"According to DS Hama's report, the usual patrol were working their beat," she replied, opening the file she'd carried in with her and scanning the top page. "In fact, from what I see here, Officer LaCosta spied your own carriage pulling out of the Rand estate shortly after twenty-eight hundred hours. Is this correct?" She glanced up.

"It is," Killian said. "The Rands hosted a gathering yesterday evening."

"And did you see anyone or anything suspicious as you departed?"

"It never occurred to me to look." Killian sniffed. "Though it shouldn't matter, should it? I was given to understand your officers had the killer dead to rights and lost him."

"There is a suspect, and he did flee the scene," Salla agreed, her eyes returning to the report. "He was identified by Msr Celia Rand as an ex-convict by the name of Gideon Quinn." She looked up. "You wouldn't happen to know a Gideon Quinn, would you, Minister?"

Killian's thoughts flashed to the Gideon he'd encountered in Kit's diner and the fact that Jessup had been worried about a man named Gideon Quinn, then he did the math on being associated in any way with a murder suspect. "I can't say I've ever met anyone by that—"

"*QUINN!*" a voice bellowed from outside the office's picture window.

A voice that was followed in short order by a rock, which shattered said window, and *that* was followed by a charging mass of a man, festooned with bits of shrubbery and armed with an assortment of makeshift weapons which seemed to have started life as plumbing equipment.

The distant sounds of additional shatterings indicated this fellow wasn't breaking and entering on his own.

Salla, however, had already drawn her weapon, the files she'd been carrying fluttering to the carpet as she took aim.

"Hold on t'yer britches, Quinn!" the intruder shouted, and then he froze mid-charge. "Oy!" He glared, looking from Salla to Killian and back. "You ain't Gideon Quinn."

"True, we are not," Salla agreed amiably, though her weapon remained steady on the target. "Any particular reason you'd be looking for Msr Quinn here?"

"Because here's where he told us to come," the man said,

then, as if in afterthought, lowered the pipe wrench he'd been brandishing.

"Did he now?" Salla glanced at Killian.

"I have no idea what this means," Killian assured, grabbing a handkerchief to mop at the sweat popping out on his forehead as a single shriek echoed through the house, followed by voices raised in various levels of protest, presumably from this fellow's accomplices.

"Oy then," the intruder said, glaring at Salla's uniform, "you're the swarmin' filth!"

"That I am," Salla agreed. "And you are swarming nicked." Even as she spoke, the door behind her opened, and her aide entered with his sidearm raised.

"We are quite safe, Gorsky," Salla assured him. "But this man is to be placed under arrest for trespassing, vandalism, and intended assault."

"Weren't nothing intended," the outraged intruder groused. "I'd'a trounced Quinn for sure if he'd been here."

"You'll want to read Msr—" She paused and looked at the oaf. "I assume you have a name?"

"Wendell," the oaf muttered. "Clive Wendell."

"Read Msr Wendell his rights," Salla said to Gorsky. "And we must also declare Minister Del's home a crime scene, possibly linked to General Rand's murder."

"What?" Killian started, handkerchief falling. "I can't imagine why—"

"I am certain it's nothing more than a misunderstanding," Salla cut in. "But the fact this ruffian was invited to your home by the prime suspect in General Rand's murder, well . . ." She shrugged. "You see how it looks."

"I—"

"For now, perhaps it is best if you join me at my office, at least until after the search is complete," Salla offered.

Killian felt his bones turn to ice. "I will have your badge of office," he said under his breath. "I will see you working waste patrol for this."

"Stranger things have happened," Salla agreed calmly. "Such as a district minister facing charges of corruption. Of course, I would never make such an accusation without proof." She glanced from Killian to the ledgers sitting on his desk and back.

For once, Killian Del had no response.

It was well after two o'clock by the time Ishan Hama pulled up outside the grounds of the Rand estate with his remaining officers.

The keepers and their new charges had returned to the Elysium Inn, where the youngsters would be offered sanctuary. Tiago had gone with them, as several of the children needed medical care.

The other half of Ishan's team went back to the precinct with the Pradesh twins, who had been taking full advantage of the right to remain silent and stare sullenly at anyone in their view.

This left Ishan with officers Prudawe, Giacomo, and Hodges, as well as Mia and the draco.

Mia, to Ishan's dismay, had refused to go with the keepers, swearing she'd make her own way to the Rand house if he tried to leave her behind.

Since Ishan didn't doubt her for a moment, he decided she'd be best in his sight rather than out of it.

He was less sanguine when, upon dismounting from his cycle, three massive silhouettes emerged from the hedge surrounding the Rand property.

"I know you," he said, as the shapes became the Ohmdahl triplets. "Drunk and disorderly," he pointed at Ulf. "Assault with a bar stool," he pointed to Rolf. "General mayhem," he pointed, finally, at Freya.

"That was long ago," Freya said.

"That was last week," Ishan told her.

"As I said, long ago." She nodded decisively. "Back when we were without purpose, before Gideon Quinn gave us a job with meaning."

"Gideon Quinn did, did he?" Ishan looked from Freya to Mia.

"He needed help to set up the marks," she said with a shrug. On her shoulder, Elvis made a complicated trill, which seemed to confirm the statement.

"Not to worry," Ulf assured Ishan. "Gideon told us you are the man in charge, and we are to follow your orders."

"Good," Ishan said, resisting the urge to press a finger to his twitching left eye. "That's . . . good."

"You have our radio, yes?" Rolf asked.

"I have a radio, yes, but—"

"Sir?" Prudawe was approaching, her own radio in hand. "I just heard from Sergeant Tyree. She says—"

"A moment," Ishan held up a hand. "Listen," he said to the three Ohmdahls, looming hopefully, "I don't believe—"

"But sir," Prudawe pressed, "she says to tell you to expect—"

"Did I not just say to give me a . . . ah . . . uh . . ." Ishan faltered to silence as a military sedan pulled up next to his cycle, barely coming to a halt before a general of the Corps began to climb out.

"Kimo Satsuke, Special Operations," she introduced herself while her gaze turned from the Ohmdahls to his own officers and landed finally on Mia before she returned her attention to Ishan. "I believe your sergeant told you to expect me?"

Ishan looked at Prudawe, who cleared her throat.

"Only just now, General," he said diplomatically. "But we didn't get far. How may I be of assistance?"

Meanwhile, inside the Rand estate, the woman known as Celia Rand settled into her tub for a well-earned bath.

It had been a very trying twenty-eight hours, threading the needle between dinner parties, abductions, and murder. Not to mention the strain of playing the traumatized wife for the police.

Though if she were honest with herself, the trauma wasn't entirely forced.

She'd thought her first encounter with Gideon Quinn, in Allianza, had been a challenge, but this last meeting—she'd made a mistake, letting him see her true self.

What had she been thinking?

Obviously you weren't thinking at all, she told herself.

Harsh, she thought, but true.

Because in that horrible, overdecorated room, facing the furious, battered Gideon, she'd found herself desperate to *be* herself.

Not Celia Rand, nor even Odile, but her*self,* the woman she might have been if she hadn't been recruited by the Midasian spy masters at the tender age of seven.

Grabbing the sponge, she dipped it in the hot water and tried to pretend she hadn't come close to telling Gideon her real name.

Duty, ingrained before all, had prevailed.

Unfortunately, Gideon had once again escaped, and while she doubted anyone would believe his version of events, she was faced with the unenviable choices of staying in place and hoping to develop a new asset, or fleeing to spy another day.

She ran the sponge over one of the bruises she'd taken when Gideon knocked her over and wondered if taking another assignment, another identity, would make her feel less hollow.

Then again, it would be difficult for any assignment to make her feel more hollow than her marriage to Jessup Rand.

"Poor Jessup," she murmured, reaching for the soap. "At least what you didn't know never hurt you."

"Actually," a voice—an infuriatingly familiar voice—interrupted her chain of thought, "it kinda did."

Then Gideon ducked, barely avoiding the soap Celia automatically threw at his head.

CHAPTER 27

Perhaps later, Gideon would appreciate the memory of a wet, naked Celia surging from the bath.

In the present moment, however, he was more concerned with containing the kicking, scratching she-draco before she could do some serious damage.

As it was, he took a wicked scratch to the throat and barely avoided a knee in his most favorite part before he swept her up over a shoulder, where the punches and kicks were more annoying than dangerous.

She did, while he was reaching down for the robe she'd left on the tile floor, get her teeth into his side, which had him *this* close to letting her drop straight down onto her head.

Fortunately for Celia, Gideon needed her alive and conscious. So, while she dug her teeth in, he reminded himself it had been a gift to find the house empty of servants when he broke in, and to expect the rest of the plan to go so easily would be greedy.

With this in mind, he gritted his own teeth, slung her out of the bath and into the adjoining bedroom—already scoured of the previous night's violence—and tossed her soapy ass onto the bed, where she immediately scrambled to her knees, ready to attack again.

"Think about it," Gideon said. "I was being nice before. You come at me again, I won't be nice. I might even do what I really want to do and break your neck."

She thought about it, and while she did, he tossed the robe he still held onto her lap.

She ignored the heap of fabric as she studied his face. "You're not lying. You really would kill me."

"I can't believe you find that surprising," he said, indicating the blood seeping through his shirt.

"But it's not your first choice," she observed, sitting back on her heels. "Which means you're not here seeking revenge, so . . . what is it you want?"

"I came for my coat," he said, then nodded to her robe. "You may as well get dressed. Unless you want to catch a cold while I continue to not fall for your charms."

Interesting, he thought, that the cool spy would blush so . . . comprehensively.

She did, however, put on the robe, tying the sash with short, angry jerks.

"Happy?" she asked, biting off the word with enough violence to make it bleed.

"I'm still a long ways from happy," he said just as shortly.

"If you are speaking of the Nasa incident—"

"It wasn't an incident. It was murder."

"It was war," she shot back. "And in war, soldiers do what they must."

"Soldiers fight on the line, face to face. They don't—"

"Don't lie? Cheat? Steal?" She shook her head. "I've read your file, Colonel Quinn. Most of your career was spent behind the lines, destroying munitions, stealing supplies . . . killing Midasian interrogators. Hardly fighting the honorable fight, was it?" As she spoke, her face, her voice, her entire body softened. "We're not so different, Gideon."

"Yes, we are, and *stop that*," he ordered. "We both know you're as seductive as the proverbial road to pollution. There's no point pushing my buttons just to prove it. Which brings up another issue . . ."

"It does indeed." She looked down, then up again. "I thought you weren't interested?"

"Ha. And I'm not," he said between clenched teeth because of course he was interested.

"Of course you're interested," she said with a scary little smile.

"You," he said shortly, "are poison."

"And you a blunt instrument," she said, showing no sign of offense. "Weapons, the both of us, in service to our countries. But knowing that, why can't we—"

"Just get along?" he cut in.

"Something like that." She leaned back, so that the satin of her robe blended with the silk of the coverlet, and it seemed to Gideon she was swimming in a pool of blood.

"Just that easy?" he asked, though his voice had gone a bit rough.

"Why not?" she asked in turn, while her hands slid up the coverlet to either side, open and inviting—until her right hand slipped beneath the massed pillows at the head of the bed.

He had to give her credit; she'd almost gotten a grip on the knife hidden under the pillow before he was on top of her, his left hand tightening around her wrist until she was forced to release the needle-like weapon.

"Nice try," he said, taking custody of the blade.

"Who says I failed?" Beneath him, she relaxed. Her lips parted, and he became uncomfortably aware how little fabric was involved in the robe she wore. "I got you where I wanted, didn't I?" When he said nothing, she smiled. "Why, Gideon, I sense you're . . . conflicted."

Conflicted wasn't the word for what he was. He could *feel* every centimeter of the woman, see the flutter of her pulse at her throat.

Every breath he took was filled with her scent.

It would be so easy to rip that flimsy bit of satin aside. So easy to . . .

What the hell is wrong with you?

He blinked, then let out a curse that came out more like a growl before flinging himself away, taking the knife with him.

She sighed and curled herself to a sitting position. "Why are you so resistant?"

"Where to start? Maybe the bit where you framed me for your husband's murder—*after* I did six years hard labor because you persuaded him to frame me for treason?" His lip curled as he added, "I'd ask how you did it, but after last night and just now, I've got a pretty good idea."

She tossed her head. "Don't be crude."

"How can you say that with a straight face?" he asked. "But that's not what I meant."

She frowned. "Then what did you mean?"

"I meant that as attractive as you are, I find it improbable that simply being in the same room with you turns me into a randy teenager with the mental faculties of a dodo."

"And that's different from your norm in what way?"

"Ouch," he said mildly, before continuing. "I felt it the first time in Allianza, right before you shot that Midasian soldier. I knew it was wrong, what I was feeling for you; especially given where we were. But all you had to do was look at me and all my thoughts just," he raised his right hand and exploded his fingers outward in description of his mental state. "Then we were moving, and I mostly forgot about it."

"Funny. I forgot it as soon as it happened."

"I don't think so," he said. "Because if you had forgotten, you wouldn't have convinced your husband I assaulted you. Who'd you get to mark you up, anyway?"

She stared.

He waited.

She sighed. "Nahmin. He did a very convincing job, so much so that Jessup went quite mad. Luckily my tears, and the fear of scandal, dissuaded him from confronting you directly."

"So instead he used his position to send my company into Nasa, making me look like a traitor," Gideon finished for her. "And I bet he never once questioned what he was doing because it was you who asked him to do it."

"He loved me," she said simply.

"I'm sure he thought he did."

She raised her hands in frustration. "How is that not the same thing?"

"It's not the same thing because it wasn't him loving you. It was you *making* him love you."

Her face, usually so expressive, closed like a moonflower at sunrise. "I have no idea what you mean."

"Cut the crap, Celia. You know exactly what I mean, and you know exactly what I mean because you can *feel* it, and you can feel it because you're not just a spy, you're a sensitive."

Nahmin spied the mass of police as soon as he reached the corner of Chaucer and Canterbury, so he continued around the next block before he parked, slipped through the Muirs' back garden, then climbed over the dividing wall to the Rand estate.

He landed in the kitchen garden nestled between the

stables and the main house, where he paused to listen to the proceedings on the other side of the wall.

Which was how he learned Quinn had used the buffoonish Ohmdahl triplets to lure Rey and Ronan to the boathouse and into the waiting shackles of the Nike PD.

Fearing the worst, he raced to the house itself only to find the servants' entrance bolted, and the key broken inside the lock.

He moved around the corner and looked up to Celia's bedroom window, from which Quinn had recently escaped.

"Are you waiting for something?" Celia asked, nothing in her voice giving away the speed at which her heart was beating. "Applause? A clap of thunder? A tearful confession?"

"I don't doubt you could pull one out," Gideon replied while, she noted, keeping a healthy distance from the bed. "But like I said earlier, I just came for my coat. And maybe some answers."

"You've done such a fine job of coming up with your own answers," she said with a negligent shrug. "What could I possibly add?"

"How about why you're still active, now the war has ended?"

"The war hasn't ended," she scoffed. "It has simply moved to a different battlefield."

"I'll say." Gideon glanced at the bed, then flipped the knife he still held before pointing it her way. "So, to sum up, you, Celia Rand, are in fact the Coalition operative known as Odile."

"Fine, yes." She sat up and crossed her arms over her knees, willing to play along until . . . well, until. "You are impressed with yourself, aren't you?"

"You are also a sensitive of some flavor or other."

"Empath," she confirmed, then gasped at the rush of revulsion that erupted from Gideon. "*What?*" she asked, blinking at the sudden stinging in her eyes.

"I guess no one's ever manipulated your emotions against your will," he said, studying her.

"Of course they have," she said, her voice almost breaking as she met his gaze, saw the flicker of his surprise even as she felt it. "How do you think we were trained?"

"I guess that—training—would be necessary for maintaining a cover as deep as yours, for as long as you did," he said, and she took some pleasure in his discomfort. "Only, and I'm guessing here," he continued, "when I was released from prison, you were worried about keeping that cover; maybe wondering how poor old Jessup would react. Maybe he's starting to feel a little bit guilty about killing those six soldiers—sorry, *five* soldiers." He shrugged. "Turns out your husband failed to murder my lieutenant."

"That's not all he failed at," she said tightly.

"Guess the mourning period is over," he observed, and started to pace as he continued. "Anyway, you're worried, and being a sensitive, you'd have known you were right to worry. What to do? What to do?" He spun from the hearth and started toward the window. "Why not solve both potential problems at once? Jessup is becoming a liability, and I'm already—"

"Troublesome," she cut in, sliding to the edge of the bed. "The word you tend to inspire is 'troublesome.'"

"And I'm troublesome," he echoed, pausing in front of her. "So why not take out two dracos with one stone? Send your lackeys out to fetch me, and once they do, you drug me, murder your husband, and leave me to wake up in his blood. How am I doing so far?"

"Impressively accurate. I would pay as much as two starbucks to see you at the Circus. So accurate, in fact, I wonder if you've a touch of sensitivity as well?"

"Doubt it."

Despite the casual tone, his eyes darkened with the desire Celia kindled. Encouraged, she prodded him further, psionically stoking the fire of his need as she asked, "And why is that?"

"Sensitives in the Barrens don't do well—something about live crystal," he told her. "Something you'll be finding out, soon enough."

"No, I'm afraid I won't," she said, even as a low, mournful keen rose from outside, causing Gideon to spin towards the window.

At the same moment Nahmin swept like smoke through the billowing curtains, his blade slicing through the air between himself and Gideon.

Celia dropped to the floor, fully expecting to see Gideon falling to the carpet at her side.

What she saw instead was Nahmin's dagger rebounding off the bedpost before dropping to the carpet with a dull *thud*.

Turning, she spied a pair of long legs in rough-spun trousers, facing the window.

Looking up, she saw Gideon, his eyes glittering dangerously, his left hand extended and empty.

Her gaze tracked the direction of that hand to see Nahmin, standing just inside the window, his expression blank and her own knife lodged in his throat.

He really has that move down, she thought, remembering another Midasian in Allianza.

Even as she thought this, Nahmin's head tipped in her direction, and his mouth fell open, but no sound emerged.

Still, she felt what he felt, and surprised the both of them with the tears that wet her cheeks. "Your service will be remembered," she told him.

Her words seemed to act as scissors, for on hearing them, Nahmin's legs buckled, and he dropped to the carpet where, after a soft sigh of release, Celia felt him no more.

She blinked away the tears to see Gideon, already crouching to retrieve Nahmin's knife from where it had fallen.

"You should run now," she told him, her voice strange and flat in her own ears.

He looked up from his study of the blade. "Why?"

She stared at him, so calm, so . . . smug . . . "You've just murdered my servant. That's two men in two days, dead by your hand."

"I didn't kill your husband."

"You killed Nahmin."

"In self-defense."

"That may be true, but we both know when it comes to your word against mine, the widow of a decorated general trumps the ravings of a convicted traitor."

"Yeah," he sighed, "I guess you're right." Then he rose and crossed toward one of her display tables. "Which makes it a good thing I left this on, so the coppers could hear our conversation."

As she watched, Gideon picked up a battered military radio from amidst the cans and music boxes and ancient shoes. "Quinn to Hama," he said into the device, "did you get all that?"

"DS Hama is on the door, but rest assured, *I* got all of it," a woman's voice, dry and crisp despite the static, came over the radio.

"General Satsuke." Gideon rolled his eyes. "So glad you could make it."

"I sincerely doubt that," the general replied. "But that enlightening conversation provided more than enough to take Msr Rand into custody, if someone will unlock the door."

"We'll be right there. Over and out," Gideon said, then set the radio down and held out a hand to Celia. "Coming?"

She looked at that hand, then at Nahmin—specifically at the dagger protruding from Nahmin's throat.

She could, she was certain, have the knife out of his throat and into her own heart before Gideon could stop her.

"If you do that," she heard Gideon say, "you'll be admitting you lost."

"I *have* lost." She looked up to see him watching her. Hatred and—something else—burned in her heart.

"You've lost the battle," he agreed. "But you said it yourself, the war's not over."

His hand was still out, still waiting.

"Why do you care?" she asked.

"I don't know," he admitted, after a beat.

Being what she was, she could feel this was so.

She could only speculate on what caused the emotional conflict. "Maybe you wish to see me suffer for my crimes."

He held her gaze. "Maybe."

"Or maybe," she said, holding up her own hand and allowing him to pull her to her feet, "you've come to accept we really are much the same."

His gaze sharpened, then he looked away.

Celia took it as a triumph, small though it was, to have rendered him speechless.

CHAPTER 28

Outside the Rand townhouse, Mia watched Elvis chase pigeons over the rooftop as the suns broke free of the clouds just in time to drop below the skyline.

She didn't think the draco was hungry. It looked more like he was having fun.

For sure, he was enjoying himself more than Mia.

Oh, it had been exciting enough earlier when she'd been huddled with Prudawe and Hama at the front door, waiting for the general lady to say it was okay to go in.

And when Elvis had gone stiff and still on her shoulder, then flown straight up to the second floor, she'd gone all tingly with fear and raced out of hiding and onto the street to see the draco hovering outside the same window Gideon had jumped from that morning.

She hadn't been able to see anything amiss, but if Elvis was keening, Mia knew something bad was happening inside.

She'd raced back to the others, to tell them they needed to get inside, that Gideon was in trouble, but by then the general lady was with them, holding the radio and ordering Gideon to unlock the door.

Her heart didn't even think about slowing down until Gideon opened the door and handed the fancy lady-murderer-spy over to the police.

After that, it had been a rush of coppers and soldiers pouring in and out of the house.

Gideon had managed to give her a quick grin and a raised fist of triumph before being herded off by DS Hama and the general, leaving Mia and Elvis to their own devices.

She supposed she could just scarp.

It wasn't as if Gideon owed her anything.

One might have said he owed her his life, but having facilitated the hive out from Ellison's control, she supposed they were dead even now.

Still she remained, making designs in the gravel with her heels and watching Elvis perform a series of aerial gymnastics until the moment Ellison's shadow crossed her line of vision.

———

Gideon collapsed into a leather chair in Jessup Rand's study, stretched his legs, and closed his eyes.

He opened them again as General Satsuke and DS Hama entered the room, leaving the fresh influx of officers—both military and civilian—to search the rest of the house.

"I don't know whether to commend you, shoot you, or send you back to Morton," General Satsuke said to Gideon.

"Due respect," DS Hama cut in, "but I believe there are a few civil matters for Msr Quinn to answer for first."

"You'll have to be more specific," Gideon said, closing his eyes again.

"Certainly," Hama replied. "Would you care to hear the charges in chronological, alphabetical, or statutory order? By the way, both myself and the Chief of Police are particularly curious as to why you had a ruffian from Lower Cadbury break into Minister Del's home."

"Someone broke into Minister Del's house?" Gideon said to his eyelids. "I'm shocked."

"If Chief Salla hadn't been in Del's house at the time, the minister might have been injured, or worse."

"And that would have been a real shame," Gideon replied, thinking of Killian Del threatening to steal a young woman's child.

Hama made a strangled sound. "Listen—"

"Perhaps this is a matter best dealt with at a higher pay grade," Satsuke cut in. "In fact, Detective Sergeant, I am certain your chief and I will be able to facilitate the more complicated aspects of Msr Quinn's—situation."

"And won't that be fun?" Gideon asked, opening his eyes and pushing himself from the chair with a surprising amount of verve. "In the meantime, if you don't mind, I'm going to find my draco. And my coat."

With this, he strode from the room, intent on his purpose.

Hama looked at Satsuke, who shook her head, and the two turned for the door just as Gideon popped back, a frantic draco on his shoulder. "Has anyone seen Mia?"

It had gone full dark by the time Ellison hauled an overlarge burlap bag liberated from the Rand stables into the boathouse that had, until today, sheltered his hive.

The decrepit building was black as pitch, but for the wavering circle of light provided by the lantern Ellison carried.

The bag had ceased bucking some time back, probably to avoid falling off the stolen motorcycle but also to spare itself Ellison's heavy-handed wrath.

Once he dropped it onto the warped boards, however, it immediately commenced wriggling again, so he gave the sack a touch of the boot.

He was gratified to see the little shape curl up on itself with a soft whimper.

"There'll be more o' that if you don't mind yerself," he told it. "You savvy?"

The top of the bag gave a subdued nod.

Satisfied, he set the lamp on a crate, then opened the sack and pulled Mia out by the hair.

"You and me," he said, kicking the sacking aside, "we're gonna have us a little talk."

"About what?" she asked, arms crossed in front of her, defiance trembling in every bone.

"All kinds o' things," he said, looming over the dodger. "Like ingratitude."

"Sorry, didn't I thank you for the back of your hand last night?"

Which was enough to have him raising his hand again.

"Now, now," a dry voice reproved from the shadows near the door, "that's no way to treat your dodgers."

Ellison and Mia both froze.

"Who's there?" Ellison turned toward the voice, drawing a blade as he shifted his grip on Mia.

"Let's just say I'm a man who has had a spectacularly bad day."

Ellison angled to follow the voice. "Quinn," he guessed, just before Mia thrust an elbow into his gut. "Ease off, girl," he snapped, knocking her up against the crate.

A heartbeat later, he was ducking as something screeched and dove at his head, then sped past to knock the lantern to the floor, where it gave a last, valiant sputter before fading to black.

Ellison silently cursed the moment he'd ever set eyes on that draco.

"I hear you met Elvis already," Quinn said. "Which means you should have figured out he doesn't like people messing with kids."

A screech from the pitch dark above confirmed this.

"I also don't like when people mess with kids," Quinn continued.

Except now he was behind Ellison.

Ellison spun again, lifting Mia up as a shield and pressing the blade against her throat. "Back off, mister, if you don't wanna see how much blood's inside this little girl."

"What did I just say about messing with kids?"

"Not a kid," Ellison corrected. "A dodger. *My* dodger."

"Not anymore," Quinn told him. "Tell you what, you put her down right now, and I'll let you walk out that door."

"Or," Ellison said, "you walk out that door right now, or I give the poppet a Midasian necktie."

There was a pause, just long enough to be gratifying to the fagin.

"Huh," Gideon said at last, "it seems you have me at a disadvantage."

"Damn right, I do. So unless you want to see this bit o' gutter filth bleedin' out onna floor, you'll be handing over that draco of yours and backing outta here."

"And then you'll let Mia go?"

"Sure," Ellison lied, just as a light flashed, no more than a brief prick of brightness in the black, but enough to fill his eyes with a confusing dance of white blobs so he never saw the knife flying his way.

But he felt it.

With a gurgle of pain, Ellison dropped the girl and slumped to his knees.

His own small blade slid from numb fingers to clatter on the floor as his left hand rose to find the wedge of a knife buried in his shoulder.

He tried to speak as a deeper shade of dark filled the air in front of him but could only emit a guttural denial.

This had to be the worst pain he'd ever known.

Then the tall shadow twisted the blade out, and he realized that, no . . . *this* was the worst pain he'd ever known.

He let out a whimper while Quinn reactivated the pocket torch he'd used to blind Ellison.

He gave Ellison a look, then handed the torch to Mia.

She took the light but stared at Quinn. "You came after me."

"Of course I came after you. Well, technically, Elvis came after you and I followed him. You okay?" he asked.

She gave her head a testing shake. "I dunno." She pushed herself to her feet. "Does right pissed count as okay?"

"Under the circumstances, yes."

Ellison, through the film of pain, saw the other man's smile, a brief flash of teeth in the torch's light.

Then he saw Mia look down at him. "You gonna kill him, then?"

Ellison felt himself shrinking under that unforgiving regard.

"That," Quinn said, "is up to him."

"To *him*?" Mia glared up at Quinn.

"T-To *me*?" Ellison asked at the same time.

"It may be," Quinn said, glancing down, "that Fagin Ellison has an urge to relocate."

"M-M-Maybe?" Ellison stuttered, grasping at any possible future that had him in it.

"Far away from Nike."

"I hear Macintosh is nice this time of year," Ellison suggested.

"Farther," Gideon prompted.

"I've . . . always wanted to see Kopernik in winter?"

"In which case," Gideon said with a nod of approval, "I don't see the need for another death today."

"*Another?*" Ellison's brain stumbled over the revelation there had been *any* deaths. "No. No need. None at all," he agreed.

For her part, Mia looked as if she had another view, but then the draco swooped down from the rafters, buzzing the cringing Ellison before coming to land on her shoulder.

Mia looked at the draco, who seemed to meet her gaze and, to the fagin's desperate relief, the cold fury in her eyes abated under the draco's calm regard.

"I suppose not," she said, finally deigning to spare a glance for her newly former fagin.

"So it's all settled," Ellison said. "Soon as I liberate my hive from them keepers."

"Your hive is forfeit," Gideon said shortly, pressing the blade to Ellison's throat. "Not a one of those kids is going with you. Consider it an early retirement," he suggested with a lightness that belied the weight of the knife in his hand.

"But I'll have nothing!"

"You'll have a pulse," Gideon reminded him.

Which, as far as arguments went, Ellison had to admit was a good one.

CHAPTER 29

Later, Gideon and Mia stood on one of the river's more active piers and watched as Ellison, still with his pulse, steamed away on the *Amber Queen*.

The crew of the riverboat, including Juban, their giant friend from The Old Man and the Sea, weren't particularly impressed by the fagin but allowed that he could work off his fare to northern Allianza, which was as near to Stolichnaya as the *Queen* sailed.

Once Ellison was aboard, Gideon took Juban aside and asked which Avonian cities the *Queen* would be stopping in along the way.

As the boat followed the river's curve and out of sight, it was Mia who spoke first. "So," she said, looking up at Gideon, "now what?"

"I think that'll be up to them," Gideon said, turning to where a Corps sedan was pulling up at the end of the pier.

Scanning the vehicle, Gideon felt a tug at the corner of his vision when his eyes passed over the silhouettes in the front seat, but then General Satsuke emerged from the back, along with

DS Hama, drawing his attention from the featureless shape of the officer riding shotgun.

"I see you found our young friend," Hama called as he jogged up to the waiting trio, leaving Satsuke speaking to someone inside the car.

"I did," Gideon said before adding, "Thanks for loaning me the bike. And the torch."

Hama waved that aside. "Tiago would not have been forgiving were I to have lost his friend," he explained, offering Mia a formal little bow before turning to Gideon. "Dare I ask what became of the fagin?"

"By all means," Gideon said, "dare."

Hama glared, then sighed, then asked, "What happened to the fagin?"

"He just shipped out on the *Amber Queen*," Gideon replied.

Hama stared. "Did it not occur to you that by allowing him to escape, you are also allowing him the opportunity to set up a new hive elsewhere?"

"It did," Gideon agreed, "but as the *Amber Queen* will be stopping in Guinness in two days, I'm sure the local police will be able to collect him on your behalf." He watched the detective's jaw twitch.

"Would it not have been simpler to hold him here, that the Nike police might take him under warrant?" the detective asked.

"Simpler? Sure," Gideon said, looking out over the dark ribbon of the Avon. "But this way Ellison has two days of hope, two days to plan how he's going to start over, maybe even contemplate a return to Nike to even the score." He turned back to Hama. "And after two days of building up his ideal future, the *Queen* will dock in Guinness, and he'll find the police waiting and realize that future is never going to happen."

Gideon watched Hama absorb this, then watched the other man's lips move in a way that told Gideon he was counting.

"Perhaps," Hama finally said, "this conversation should also have never happened." At Gideon's raised eyebrow, he shrugged. "An anonymous tip will suffice for the report." As he spoke, General Satsuke stepped onto the dock. "Speaking of reports," Hama continued, "I don't see my cycle anywhere, and you've no idea what the requisition forms are like should I need a new one."

"No worries," Gideon said, tossing the key to the detective. "I parked it between the incoming cotton and outgoing steel. Mia can show you the way."

"I can?" Mia asked, giving Gideon a look of concern.

"It'll be okay," Gideon told her, glancing at the waiting Satsuke. "Elvis can go with you," he added, and a click and a gesture sent the draco hopping from his shoulder to Mia's.

As before, the draco's presence seemed to steady the girl, enough that she was willing to head out with the detective while Gideon joined Satsuke. "If you want your knife back," he said, referring to the blade she'd tossed him on his way out, "you might want to wait until all the fagin's been cleaned off."

"Consider it a spoil of war," she replied, not missing a beat. Then she simply stood, hands clasped behind her, watching him.

"So," Gideon began, echoing Mia's earlier query, "now what?"

"That is a loaded question," Satsuke replied, staring at Gideon long enough for him to wonder if he should have gotten on the *Amber Queen* with Ellison. "But to begin," she continued at last, "there is this." And as she spoke, she pulled from behind her back a lump of fabric which, when Gideon took it, turned out to be his coat.

"You found it," he said, then cleared his throat.

"One of my officers did," Satsuke told him. "It was in a chest hidden behind a false wall of her closet, along with a few other —souvenirs—from Odile's various conquests. A lucky discovery for us," she continued, "as many of those items are unique enough to be traced to her assets."

"Assets or victims?" Gideon asked. "Given Celia's abilities, manipulating emotions the way she did, they didn't stand much of a chance."

"They had as much chance as you," Satsuke pointed out. "And though I take your point, the fact remains that every single one of those people has been compromised by a foreign agent. We have to know what they told her."

Since there wasn't much Gideon could say to that, he opted to put on his coat, settling it over his shoulders and, for the first time since settling into that tub at the Elysium, felt himself fully relax.

Though if he were really being honest, he hadn't been truly relaxed for close to seven years, but that was just too depressing to dwell on, especially now that Odile had been uncovered and his name cleared.

Assuming his name *had* been cleared.

He looked up to see Satsuke watching him, and her expression said she'd not only followed his entire thought process but anticipated it.

"There is also this," she said, holding out a folded document, several pages thick and bearing the seals of the Corps Special Operations and United Colonial Judicial System.

He looked from the document to the general but didn't reach out for it.

He was, perhaps, less relaxed than he'd originally thought.

"Trust me," she said, "you'll want to take it."

He wasn't so sure he trusted her, but he did take it.

Holding his breath, he broke the seals.

It was a long time before he let that breath out.

"It's a bit late, but I hope you will accept this full acquittal and the accompanying reinstatement of your rank and all honors earned in the service of the United Colonies," General Satsuke said formally while Gideon continued to stare at the document. "There is also a provision for six years of back pay, to be delivered upon your acceptance of the terms."

"Terms?" he asked, staring at the repeal of every crime for which he'd been convicted, all laid out in black and white. Then he looked up.

"The unwritten terms," she said.

"Which are?"

"No one can know the truth about Odile."

CHAPTER 30

There was a pause in which Gideon, uncertain he'd heard correctly, stared, then shook his head. "That's a joke, right? Tell me you're joking."

"I don't do jokes," she told him, then held up a hand to forestall the protest he was already forming. "Hear me out," she began. "You know the war is over, and for the most part in our favor."

"Because we won," he said.

"On paper, yes," she agreed. "But imagine what would happen to our very new and very delicate peace if it came out that a Midasian agent had not only been siphoning intelligence from under the Corps' nose for at least twelve years but was *still doing so*? The public wouldn't stand for it, which means the Colonial Congress would demand action—sanctions at best and renewed conflict at the worst."

"Which is bad," Gideon admitted, "but do we really want to negotiate with a power that, by their own spy's admission, doesn't think the war is really over?"

"No one in the trade thinks the war is really over," she told him. "Shadow wars never end. What we can't risk is a renewal of armed hostilities, and we can't risk it," her voice went flat, "because the cold truth is, if we were to take to the field at our current strength, we would lose."

"Wait," he began. "I read the news reports—Esa was huge for us."

"It was," she agreed. "But that battle also cost us dearly. The best that can be said is that the retaking of Esa led the Coalition to believe we were in better shape than they, so they sued for peace."

Which was not what Gideon expected, or wanted, to hear. "What are the chances," he asked, "that Odile has already passed that information on?"

"I've considered that, but General Rand had only just been assigned to Tactical; that is, he was not in a position to know how precarious our situation was, at the end."

"And if he had, and Celia had alerted her superiors, the Coalition would have taken action by now," Gideon concluded.

"That is our hope, at least."

Gideon nodded, though it all felt a little optimistic. "We were really losing?"

"One more major engagement—two at the most—and the eastern territories would have begun to fall like dominoes."

"And what about them?" Gideon nodded to where DS Hama and Mia were rolling his cycle to a stop under the pier's lamp. "Do they have to keep Odile a secret too?"

"They weren't privy to Msr Rand's confession and only know what I shared, which isn't much."

Gideon nodded. "So, if I can't talk about Odile, what are we saying happened at Nasa?"

"It was a crime of passion," she said, the relief in her voice unnerving as it highlighted to Gideon how precarious the

Colonies' position must be. "Celia Rand, in revenge for your refusal of her advances, misled her husband into believing you had assaulted her, leading to his actions at Nasa. Tawdry, I'll admit, but close enough to the truth that we should be able to make it fly."

"Make it fly?" Gideon said. "Twenty starbucks say it'll be on the center stage at the Circus within the month."

"I don't believe I will take that bet," she said with a small smile, which quickly disappeared as she asked, "And will you do it? Will you keep this secret? I can't say the Corps deserves your silence, but—"

"I won't talk," Gideon assured. "Anyway, I'm not sure my truth sounds any more plausible than your fiction."

Her smile returned, and as one, they turned toward the dock and started walking. "At least you'll have your freedom, and your reputation."

But not those six years, he thought. *And those five soldiers are still dead.*

He didn't let himself think of Dani.

"You also have your rank," Satsuke offered, almost as if responding to his thoughts, and he wondered if perhaps the general had a little sensitivity of her own. "That is, if you want it. The Corps still needs people who think . . . differently."

By now they were at the landward end of the pier. On the dock to Gideon's left waited Mia with DS Hama, and to his right, the general's staff car.

Her driver was already at the door, holding it open.

It would certainly be easy to accept Satsuke's offer.

After all, his entire life had been one of following orders. Dodger, soldier, convict . . .

As he thought this, a fine rain began to fall, and he thought of stepping off the *Ramushku* the day before, carrying little but his anger, a draco, and a whole lot of doubt.

"Thanks," he said, pausing at the foot of the pier to meet the general's gaze. "It means something you'd make the offer, but I don't think this is the kind of war I'm cut out to fight. In fact," he added, looking out over the city, "I think I'm due for a career change."

"What sort of change?" Satsuke asked.

"Uncertain," Gideon replied, considering the question.

He could always take ship, like Horatio Alva, and see where he landed. Or do as Jinna had when she left the Corps and find a nice normal job.

His thoughts danced over to the *Errant* and Pitte's crew, but even if Jagati didn't shoot him on sight, there was a bit too much history there.

He looked at Hama and thought, *copper?*

But no, too many regulations. And if there was one thing Gideon was sure of, he was through taking orders.

He thought again of Jinna, the troubles with Minister Del, and of what he'd learned of Nike's politics, then he looked at DS Hama, a decent cop in a very not decent system, then of Tiago and the issues in Lower Cadbury.

"I'll think of something," he determined as they joined Hama and Mia.

"Something for what?" Mia asked.

"Colonel—pardon me—*Msr* Quinn is having something of a career crisis," Satsuke told her.

Mia opened her mouth.

"I'm trying to decide what to do with my life," Gideon explained.

"Oh," Mia said, "that's easy. You can do what you been doing since you got here."

Hama looked a little panicked, and Gideon couldn't blame him.

"You can facilitate," Mia explained.

Gideon, who'd been ready to protest, shut his mouth.

He looked at Mia, then at Elvis, curled around the girl's neck, and then, for no reason he could fathom, to the shadow in the front seat of the general's car.

"I could," he said after a moment, turning back to Mia. "I could absolutely . . . facilitate."

The general blinked. "I wasn't aware such a career existed."

"Gideon just invented it." Mia beamed.

"First landers preserve me," Hama sighed. "The paperwork you have generated in one night will keep me busy for a month."

Mia patted his arm. "It won't always be that bad, and you got five right wasps inna nick in one night too."

Hama appeared to brighten at this thought.

"You're sure about this?" General Satsuke asked Gideon.

Gideon tried on the idea, discovered he liked the fit. "Surprisingly, yes."

"Then I wish you well," she said. "May the Corps' loss be Nike's gain." She turned on her heel and started for her vehicle, but after three steps stopped and turned back. "Tell me, as a private—facilitator—would you be open to the occasional military contract?"

His head tilted as he felt a surge of something too new to recognize. "That depends."

"On what?"

Gideon's teeth flashed in not quite a grin. "On whether I like the job."

"Fair enough." She nodded. "Goodbye, Msr Quinn. For now."

Satsuke turned again, this time not stopping until she reached the staff car.

She climbed in and waited for the corpsman to close the door, take his seat, and start the engine before she spoke to the officer sitting shotgun. "You were right. He's not coming back to the Corps."

The captain nodded, though she continued to watch Gideon, who was speaking to the detective and the girl.

"I wonder, though," Satsuke continued, also watching Gideon, "if he'd have made the same choice, had I let him know *you* were the officer who made his freedom a possibility?"

"I don't have to wonder," Captain Indani Solis, whom Gideon had always called Dani, replied. "He would have returned. Out of gratitude, he would have come back."

Now her eyes dropped to her left hand and the wedding band that graced it. "I don't see that working out well for any of us."

Outside, Gideon, Mia, and Hama waited for the general's car to drive off before turning for the city.

Once the car departed, they set off, Hama walking his cycle while Mia perched on the seat and Elvis perched on Mia.

As they made their meandering way from the riverfront, Mia continued to regale the men with plans for Gideon's new business, from where to set up shop—near to but not *in* Lower Cadbury, she determined—to the type of jobs he should take, to what sort of advertising would best serve Nike's first ever Private Facilitator.

Hama, for his part, continued to intersperse which laws and statutes would have to be observed to keep Gideon out of the nick and, more importantly, paperwork off Hama's desk.

Gideon, amused, let them wrangle over the details.

For himself, he was perfectly happy to make it up as he went along.

Six years' back pay from the Corps wouldn't quite elevate him to the level of a risto, but it would provide a significant cushion.

Enough to keep himself and Elvis, and—he glanced sideways at the animated dodger on the bike—his assistant, fed and under a roof while he worked it out.

In the meantime, he was, for the first time in memory, free to do as he chose.

Chances were what he chose would be messy, skating the edges of legality and, if the past thirty hours were any indication, worthy of at least the box theatre at the Circus.

It would also, almost certainly, be interesting.

And who knew, while he was making interesting messes, he might also manage to help a few people out. People like Jinna and Tiago and—*admit it, Quinn*—himself.

People the system had somehow overlooked, or left behind, or simply turned its back on.

He thought all of that as he walked along with Mia and the detective, and then he thought maybe they should grab some grub, as he was at least a quarter past starving, and Elvis was looking a bit gray as he hunched away from the despised rain.

He thought about how to find homes for the dodgers currently sheltering with the keepers at the Elysium, and whether the Ohmdahls had gotten their radio back, and what sort of charges Killian Del might be facing.

Which made him think they should get word to the *Errant* that it was safe for Jinna to return to Nike if she chose (possibly breaking Rory's heart), and if she did, what were the chances of her still having a job to return to?

The one thing he didn't do, as they turned onto the main road to the city, was count how many steps he was taking.

Look for more Gideon Quinn in *Fortune's Fallen* and *Fortune's Fool*.

And turn the page for a sneak peek at *Outrageous Fortune* and the *Errant* crew's job-gone-wrong.

PREVIEW: OUTRAGEOUS FORTUNE

FORTUNE CHRONICLES 2

PROLOGUE

UCAS Kodiak
Approaching Nasa Escarpment
Treicember 21, 1442 After Landing

CAPTAIN JOHN PITTE ENTERED THE BRIDGE OF THE *KODIAK* with blood on his hands and fury in his eyes. He tried to control his limp, but every step he took felt as if his knee were stabbing itself from within.

Someday, he'd have to see about getting that shrapnel removed.

"Captain on bridge!" Sergeant Millar, the duty provost, announced.

"As you were," John said, brushing past the prov, his steps thudding unevenly on the deck as he approached the command dais where General Jessup Rand had stationed himself, hands clasped behind his back and attention fixed on the Nasa Escarpment, which loomed ever larger through the forward windows.

John, crossing the deck, took a deep breath of the familiar

allusteel and oil mix, slightly tainted by the coppery odor of blood he brought with him. He felt the deck inclining slightly as the helm adjusted the *Kodiak*'s altitude.

Other than the thrum of the engines and accompanying clanks, pings, and clicks of the airship's workings, the bridge was quiet.

John was within a few steps of the dais when Rand finally turned to acknowledge his presence. Eyebrows rising, the general stepped away from the forward rail and crossed to the aft steps.

"Captain."

"General." John continued until he reached the foot of the dais.

Rand's dark face tipped down, then up. "You appear to be injured."

"Bad turn on the ladder," John said, looking up at Rand. As he did, he noticed a shadow emerging from the far side of the dais.

A shadow which resolved itself into Sergeant Jihan, General Rand's aide de camp.

"That was fast," John said to Jihan, whom he'd left on the *Kodiak*'s lowest deck not fifteen minutes past.

Jihan offered a salute but said nothing, adding to the heavy silence of the bridge, which pressed on John from all sides in a way utterly unfamiliar to him.

Possibly because it was no longer *his* bridge, not in any way that mattered, not with Rand in control of the *Kodiak* and the helm, elevator, and nav all being operated by Rand's officers.

Even Millar, the duty prov who'd called John's presence, had come aboard with the general currently studying John's uniform with obvious distaste.

Perhaps Rand objected to the sight of blood.

"You are out of uniform, Captain," Rand said, confirming John's supposition.

"And your man is out of order, General," John replied, his eyes darting to where Jihan stood at the foot of the dais. "Provost Millar," he called over his shoulder, "please place Sergeant Jihan under warrant for assault and conduct unbecoming a member of the Corps."

"Belay that, Millar," Rand called over John's shoulder. "Captain." He stepped forward but remained on the dais. "As I am certain Jihan would have told you, he was acting on my orders. It was your man, McCabe, whose behavior called for punishment."

"Punishment," John repeated.

"For dereliction of duty," Jihan inserted at the general's nod.

John didn't look at the sergeant. "Assuming I believe that, which I don't, since when did the Colonial Corps adopt the Coalition's use of the lash?"

"Since the dereliction in question endangered an entire airship," Rand countered.

"Gunner's Mate McCabe failed to report a faulty containment cell in one of his cannons," Sergeant Jihan inserted so promptly it struck John as rehearsed. "If I hadn't noticed the damage, the *Kodiak* might have been lost with all hands."

"You do get around," John murmured, sparing the general's aide a cold glance.

"My aide knows I like a full picture."

John turned back to Rand. "If such negligence occurred, it would still call for a full investigation and the convening of a court-martial, not the draco's tail in the cargo bay with no witnesses."

Rand's eyebrows rose. "I'd suggest you calm yourself, Captain Pitte."

"I believe myself to be quite calm," John said, briefly taken aback. He'd not raised his voice once, except to get Millar's attention.

"In that case you might, in your cool-headedness, recall that a commander has the right to enact field justice in a time of war."

"And as I am McCabe's commander, it was my right to make that determination," John reminded the general . . . calmly. "Yet somehow neither these accusations nor this—field justice—came to my attention. Had my first officer not come across McCabe being dragged below decks, I'd still not have known."

Even as he said this, John saw something flash in the general's expression, something like satisfaction.

"And I remind *you*," Rand said, "that for the duration of this mission, a mission that involves recovering an entire company of deserters, the *Kodiak* and her crew are mine to command."

"With respect," John said, "in all matters *not* relating to your mission, such as the day-to-day running of the *Kodiak*, the 'ship and crew are *my* responsibility, and that includes all matters of crew performance."

And there John spied it, again, that flash of satisfaction in the other man's expression.

"It pains me to admit, but you may be correct, Captain Pitte," Rand said, glancing at Jihan, who nodded and stepped from his position to stand behind John. "Mr. McCabe is of your crew, which makes him your responsibility and *your* failure. As such, I am compelled to order the surrender of your command—"

"Excuse me?" John stepped forward.

"—until such time as a full inquiry determines the level of your complicity in your crew's negligence," Rand continued, nodding at his aide.

Jihan reached for John's sword, but John snatched the sergeant's wrist. "No," he said quietly.

"Don't make this difficult, sir," Jihan said.

"Captain," Moncivais called from the radio alcove, "I'm receiving word of groundside movement from the crow's nest."

John shoved Jihan away. "What kind—"

"What kind of movement?" Rand cut in. "Where on the ground?"

Moncivais looked at John, who gave a short nod, and turned to Rand. "Sir, crow's nest reports spying several individuals at the top of the Nasa Escarpment. She can't make a positive ID as the suns are setting, but they are there, and armed."

"The deserters. Just as I expected," Rand said. "Radio." He turned to Moncivais. "Contact Commander O'Bannion and tell her to have her jump teams standing by." As he spoke, he flipped the command intercom, set into the dais, to life. "This is General Rand to gunner deck. Charge all cannons and prepare to fire."

"*Cannons charging, aye,*" a tinny voice emerged from the speaker.

"Belay those orders," John called, earning a scathing glance from Millar and a confused "Sir?" from Moncivais.

"*Say again?*" came from the dais speaker.

"Did I hear you correctly, *Captain?*" Rand looked over his shoulder. "Do as you were ordered," he said to both the speaker and Moncivais before focusing on John. "You are treading on dangerous ground, Captain Pitte."

"Perhaps. But it strikes me odd that a company of alleged deserters would be standing in clear view of one their own airships."

"We're being hailed," Moncivais announced.

John, Rand, and even Sergeant Jihan turned to the radio operator.

"Put it on speaker," John ordered, ignoring Rand's hiss as Moncivais flicked the speakers to life.

"*—hailing UCAS* Kodiak *under Captain Pitte, this is Corpsman Carver, 12th Company, 96th Infantry, please respond . . .*"

"It's them," Rand said, his satisfaction palpable. "We have him."

"We have a contact," John corrected. "Request the colonel's ident for verification," he said to Moncivais. "And to specify the nature of his mission."

"Jihan," Rand said.

Just that—just *Jihan*—and before John could blink he felt it, the cold intrusion of steel into flesh. He looked down to see the point of Jihan's sword emerging above his right hip.

"Consider yourself relieved of duty," Jihan murmured in his ear, then yanked the sword out.

The force of the weapon's removal caused John to jerk back, which caused his head to bounce up, so he caught sight of Moncivais, already half risen from her chair. He had enough strength to shake his head at her—*no point.*

"*Repeat, UCAS* Kodiak *this is Corpsman Carver, 12th Company, do you read? Over.*"

John shook his head again as he heard Rand delivering targeting orders to the cannon.

"Captain John Pitte," the Jihan intoned formally, "you are hereby placed under warrant . . ."

"All cannons take aim," Rand said.

"*Repeat, repeat, Captain Pitte . . .*" the young voice continued to call over the speakers.

"*Cannons taking aim, aye.*"

"You can't," John said.

Rand didn't even spare him a glance. "I already have," he said as another voice crackled over the speaker.

"Hey, Kodiak, *this is Colonel Gideon Quinn, 12th Company. Do you read? Over."*

"Prepare to fire on my mark," Rand snapped into the radio as he stared through the windows at the escarpment.

"Repeat, repeat, Captain Pitte . . ."

I'm here, John said—or rather, thought he said.

"Mark," Rand said.

Don't, John thought, even as the whine of the plasma cannons filled the air.

John looked down at the thrumming deck, noting as he did the dark red drops vibrating as they fell, and then he too was falling. And then he was on the deck, the cold metal against his cheek contrasting with the warm blood seeping from his uniform.

Lying there, unable to move or speak, he heard Carver's voice again hailing him and then, last of all . . .

"All cannons, fire at will." Rand's voice, dark with triumph, followed John into the sanguine fog.

CHAPTER 1

JOHN DUCKED A SIZZLING BOLT OF PLASMA, STRAIGHTENED, and glanced at the smoking hole left in the multihued strata for which Dyar's Canyon was renowned.

Admittedly, Dyar's Canyon was also renowned for its inhospitable fauna, alkali lakes, and treacherous electrical storms, but John felt a perverse fondness for the place. It was dangerous and beautiful and defiant and didn't give a lick for the humans who'd created it.

"What the fecking comb are you waiting for?" Jagati O'Bannion, John's first mate, asked as she ran past.

"Sorry," he said, racing after her, "but these people have no respect for nature."

"Report it to the keepers," she called over her shoulder as a series of shouts, followed by more plasma bursts, had both laying a quick burst of suppressive fire before slipping single file through the jagged fissure.

"Come on, come on, come on!" Jagati hissed as she clambered over a tumble of fallen stone.

"I'm come onning," John replied, one hand on the satchel he wore crosswise over his jacket.

He'd almost reached the top of the rock pile when another shot had him diving the rest of the way over, resulting in an awkward rolling-falling-bruising affair. He continued to roll to his feet with a fresh spate of twinges. "It's entirely possible," he panted, "that taking this job was a mistake."

From the steady stream of epithets drifting back his way, he could only assume Jagati shared his opinion.

"—ing, smog-eating, spawn of a hornet," she finished as he came even with her.

A sideways glance showed the raw umber of her skin matted with the same violet grime which coated their clothes and dusted the spiraling mass of her brown-black curls. Combined with her fierce expression, the end result was rather demonic.

At least she looked threatening.

If the back of his hand was any indication, John figured he came off like a victim of some unnamed, wasting disease.

"We're close to the LZ, right?" she asked, slowing as the canyon they traversed narrowed to the width of an airship's crawlspace.

"Almost certainly," he agreed, nudging her onward while he removed the satchel and held it at his side so he could fit through the cramped fissure.

"Almost?" Stuck sideways with her head turned forward, he could only imagine her glare. "*Pitte.*"

"Best keep moving," he prompted.

She hissed but kept moving, and in a few minutes which

passed like only a few years, they squeezed through to the other side, where Jagati came to a halt and scanned the wider space.

"Pitte," she said again, which in Jagati shorthand meant *Tell me we're not lost. And if you can't tell me we're not lost, at least tell me we have a plan to become unlost. And if we don't have a plan to become unlost, feel free to present your ass for me to kick all the way back to the shadow traders' camp.*

Jagati's shorthand was an incredible time saver.

"We're not lost," he told her.

"Good."

"Except I think we should already have passed the column that looks like a mammoth's—"

"*Pitte!*"

"Oh, there it is." He pointed to the right, where the cold blaze of the noontime suns had flattened the distinctive geographic feature.

"Overcompensation," Jagati muttered, even as a rapid series of plasma bursts cut the suggestive formation down to size.

She ducked, glanced back, and cursed anew as a shadow trader emerged from the crevice.

"Almost there," John assured, ignoring the smoke curling up from a fresh plasma score on his right thigh.

"Can't be soon enough." She jogged past him, then paused. "Smog it, Pitte, you're—"

"Heads!" he warned.

She ducked, spun, and fired on the foremost outlaw. When the distant shape let out a short squeal and dropped, she backed up and tucked herself under John's shoulder.

Thus linked, they turned and ran for it while John fired off an occasional shot at their pursuers.

"That's the last tunnel." He jerked his chin forward, toward an inverted V of a passage which connected to the canyon where they'd left their airship moored.

An airship their crewmates should have fired up and ready to fly the second John and Jagati hit the gangplank.

She nodded and urged him faster. "This is more resistance than I expected. Do we even know what it is we're retrieving?"

"The client chose not to disclose that information." He disengaged his arm from her shoulder and limped into the tunnel. "When I asked, she said it was sensitive and started to cry."

"I hate when they cry," she said as she followed him into the passage. "Wait! I mean, don't wait, but . . . the client's a *she?*"

"Of course. Didn't I say?"

"Nooo . . ."

"Ah. Well, then, yes—the client is a woman," he said. "Typical spoiled risto with more money than sense. I've no doubt we're risking life and limb for her great-grandmother's 7-Up reliquary."

"Could be worse," Jagati said. "Could be another one of those ancient torture devices."

"That was a shoe. An original Louboutin, as I recall."

"You say shoe, I say spiky pain-delivery device."

"At any rate," he said, "whatever is in this satchel meant enough for the client to offer treble the usual fee for a recovery."

"It's not enough."

John didn't reply but limped faster, bracing a hand against the side of the cavern until he stepped out into the bright light of day . . . and froze in his tracks.

Behind him, Jagati came rushing out, only stopping when she ran into his back.

"What's wrong?" she asked, squeezing past him. "Shouldn't we be boarding about now?"

"It was here," he said, staring at the wide, flat, and—most importantly—empty space before them. "It was right *here.*" He peered up, shielding his eyes from the suns, and Jagati followed suit.

"Smogging toxic Earth!" Jagati stomped her foot, raising a puff of purple dust. "This! Isn't! Funny!" She ran forward into the empty place once occupied by their vessel, then she—yes—cursed some more.

"Feel better?" John asked, limping up to join her.

Her lip curled in a snarl. "What do you think?"

"Just asking," he said, giving the tunnel they'd emerged from a meaningful glance.

She growled, then gave him a punch on the shoulder, then led the way to a craggy outcropping at the base of the canyon's northern wall. "I will kill them," she muttered as she began to climb. "I will kill them and dance in their blood. I may be sorry, later, but I'll do it."

John almost smiled but knew better than to say anything.

"Here," she called down, "toss me the case."

He unslung the leather carryall and heaved it up.

Jagati caught the strap and slung the bag over the top edge of the ridge. "There's level ground up here," she called down. "And it's defensible. Sort of."

He nodded and started to climb after her, but stopped cold at a sudden rattling of stone from the canyon wall to his right. Turning, he clung to the face with one hand and shaded his eyes with the other as he searched for the sound's origin.

What he saw made him release his grip on the outcropping and drop back to the canyon floor, where his leg almost buckled under him.

"What the hell are you doing?" Jagati asked from on high.

John, in the act of raising his hands, jerked his chin upwards.

As he had, she shielded her eyes from the suns and stared in the indicated direction.

There was a telling silence from above. It told him Jagati had also spied the sniper perched at the canyon's upper edge.

<hr>

Outrageous Fortune is now available.

Follow our Outrageous Crew on Ream for free to read the short story, *A Soldier is Born*, introducing Gideon at a crucial turning point in his youth.

As a follower, you will find complete novels, new stories, exclusive to Ream content and fellow lovers of quirky science fantasy.

Scan the QR code below to begin reading!

Acknowledgments

First of all, **thanks to you,** for reading this book.

Without you, Gideon's determination, Mia's courage, and Elvis's cleverness would be for nought, so give yourself a round of applause.

In addition, many thanks to Lori Drake and Cameron Coral for the morning writing/editing sessions, as well as Claudette Cruz, Lori Diederich, and Youness Elh for making *Soldier of Fortune* readable and pretty, respectively. And of course a huge round of applause for Kelley McKinnon, my partner in Fortune and the dramaturge of this ever-expanding world.

Thanks to the fam, original and chosen (and more spread out than when we started), but still providing sympathy, cheers, and hugs as needed. I love you all beyond the telling.

About the Author

As a lifelong fan of complex characters and outrageous worlds, I lean on my history in theatre, fight choreography, and parenting to create immersive adventures, engaging characters, and unlikely partnerships (because I pretty much live for oddballs teaming up against a bad system).

I can also be found hanging out at Ream Stories, growing more outrageous adventures featuring flawed heroes, chosen families, and all the snark you care to entertain.*

*__True story:__ In first grade, my youngest turned in a daily journal entry featuring the opening phrase, "Sometimes, my mommy can be sarcastic."**

**I've never felt more seen.